PRAISE FOR COLD

"*Cold* is an atmospheric, tightly woven murder mystery
told with a sharp voice and a complex, layered cast.
The kind of story you inhale."

—**RANDY RIBAY**, AUTHOR OF THE NATIONAL BOOK
AWARD WINNER *PATRON SAINTS OF NOTHING*

"Mariko Tamaki's *Cold* is a sharply written, moody
mystery/noir in which even the ghosts have
something to hide. Will give you chills."

—**LAURA RUBY**, TWO-TIME NATIONAL BOOK AWARD FINALIST
AND AUTHOR OF *THIRTEEN DOORWAYS, WOLVES BEHIND THEM ALL*

"Tamaki brilliantly explores the ways we show up for each
other and the ways we don't. A rare, unforgettable mystery
about finding the truth inside yourself, despite loss."

—**GWENDA BOND**, *NEW YORK TIMES*–BESTSELLING AUTHOR

"In *Cold*, Mariko Tamaki creates a world of kids crashing
into adulthood with writing that is gritty and moving. This is
a story where the living sometimes haunt us more than ghosts.
Tamaki dazzlingly shows us that the search for love and justice
can be more tangled up than we realize."

—**EMILY SCHULTZ**, AUTHOR OF *THE BLONDES* AND *LITTLE THREATS*

COLD

ALSO BY MARIKO TAMAKI

Skim

This One Summer

Saving Montgomery Sole

Laura Dean Keeps Breaking Up with Me

COLD

MARIKO TAMAKI

ROARING BROOK PRESS

NEW YORK

Published by Roaring Brook Press
Roaring Brook Press is a division of Holtzbrinck Publishing Holdings
Limited Partnership

120 Broadway, New York, NY 10271 • fiercereads.com

Library of Congress Cataloging-in-Publication Data is available.

ISBN 978-1-62672-273-6

Our books may be purchased in bulk for promotional, educational, or
business use. Please contact your local bookseller or the Macmillan Corporate
and Premium Sales Department at (800) 221-7945 ext. 5442 or by email at
MacmillanSpecialMarkets@macmillan.com.

First edition, 2022 • Book design by Trisha Previte
Skull emoji © by Carboxylase/Shutterstock

Printed in the United States of America

10 9 8 7 6 5 4 3 2 1

FOR MY FAMILY.

COLD

GEORGIA
THE STORY OF ME

THE FIRST STORY OF ME was written by my mother when I was four years old.

(Before I had any idea that it was possible to have a story of me, or an agent representing my interests.)

The book is called *I Am Little and You Are Big*. It is a bestseller. You have probably seen it in some kid's toy box or in a display of books at your local bookstore. Maybe you read it when you were little and loved it.

In the book, which a reputable reviewer described as an "inventive and compelling retelling of 'Hansel and Gretel,'" I am the little sister, Molly, lost in the woods with my older brother, Wally, the stand-in for my older brother, Mark.

The whole book is little me asking my big brother

what things are. So I'm constantly like, "What is that?" and "Where are we going?"

In the book, Wally aka Mark just answers all my questions.

"What is that?"

"That is the moon."

"What is THAT?"

"That's a tree."

I'm four and I don't know what a tree is?

At one point in the book, I ask my big brother why he knows all this stuff and he says, "Because you are little and I am big."

Maybe it's not shocking that I'm not a fan of this book. Among the many my mother has published and the MULTITUDE that are basically about me, it is my least favorite. Partly because a book where a girl is walking around the woods clueless is not really the most modern retelling of the existing fairy tale (even if in this one the witch turns out to be nice and no one is threatened with getting eaten).

There's also the fact that I spent a solid year of my life dressed up as the "me" of this book, in a little yellow dress and matching shoes and bonnet, going to bookstores and eating warm snack trays of cantaloupe and crackers and cheese, which does something to a person, if only turn them off cantaloupe forever.

Maybe I don't like this book because it's not me and yet somehow it's me.

It's like I never got a shot at being anything else.

Sometimes I feel like I'm standing in the woods, all covered in snow, and there's already a set of footprints, somehow my footprints, that I've somehow already stomped into the ground without knowing it, a path I already walked stretching out in front of me.

And, really, most of the time I feel like I am lost, and all I want to do is ask questions.

TODD
TODD MAYER IS COLD AS ICE

A LIGHT HAZE OF SNOW fell on Rosemary Peacock Park on the morning of January 21.

Originally named for some long-ago dead white guy, in the late '90s the park was rededicated to a more recently deceased local resident, Rosemary Peacock, devoted dog lover and city rich person. By February, the park was typically, as it was on this night, a sea of frozen paw prints and left-behind tiny dog shits, melted and refrozen over and over.

On the far west side of the park was a kids' playground, with a set of swings, a pair of climbable abstract shapes on giant springs, and a towering rope spiderweb for aspiring spiders.

On the south end, the grass edge of the dog park dipped down into a ravine.

The ravine was a place for people who didn't want to be seen, with trees just thick enough to hide a kid smoking a cigarette, or a secret.

A secret like the increasingly frozen and very dead body of Todd Mayer.

Todd Mayer floated above the park, thinking about the fact that he was dead and how this was a generally tragic thing.

Because dying young is tragic, no matter who it is.

The thing about being dead, Todd knew, was that it was at least preferable to the state of dying.

Dying, in Todd's experience, was horrible, probably the worst thing that could happen to a person.

The last and worst thing.

Todd knew symptoms of hypothermia: Hunger. Nausea. Apathy. Core body temperature drop. Confusion. Lethargy. Loss of consciousness.

To save someone from hypothermia, a rescuer should throw a blanket over the victim, remove the victim's clothes, and wrap themselves, naked, around the victim's body.

When Todd first heard this piece of first aid trivia, he was in grade nine, in health class. He remembered watching Mr. Sterman, with his tight slacks and velvety voice, and thinking about skin and ice. A dangerous thing to think about when you're in health class.

Todd couldn't help but think the whole thing sounded romantic, like some sort of Nordic art film, like the movies he was just starting to watch at retro cinemas, alone and for strictly academic purposes.

Then the boy who sat behind him in health took a moment to lean forward in his desk and hiss,

"Looks like you're going to die with some frooozen balls, homo!"

This was grade nine, before Todd learned to stop his cheeks from flushing, before he learned to make his face a mask, and so the heat rose up into his face and made his eyes water.

The ghost of Todd hovered over his now dead face and considered the features that used to annoy him that now just seemed to exist. His big nose. His sunken eyes. His thick black hair that would never take a shape or hold a haircut, that stuck to the sides of his forehead.

Todd took a moment to take in the scar where he fell and hit his chin on the stairs when he was twelve. The zit on his bottom lip that he'd noticed two days ago but left alone because he figured he could press on it all day and it would get big and juicy and be easier to pop when he got home.

Now that zit would be on his face forever. Or at least until his body rotted into the ground and became enzymes or whatever bodies become before they become dirt.

The idea of being dirt was soothing to Todd, not that any of this, this being dead stuff, was particularly upsetting.

It just . . . was.

The sun came up. A beam hit Todd's nose, a pinprick of light. Like that scene where Pinocchio becomes a real boy. Todd watched the sun crawl up into the sky, changing it from mauve to a hazy blue. His first day being dead.

A black-and-white dog with a blue collar darted down into the ravine. It barked and jumped over the snowbank next to Todd's body. It lowered its nose into the snow and sniffed around Todd's head, then it dug a paw into the snow beside his ear.

Todd looked at his body again and noticed that his body was naked.

The dog barked and dodged down to Todd's arms, where it resumed digging. And barking.

Todd mayer is cold as ice.

The joke started sometime after the health class in grade nine. A multifaceted insult, as all good insults should be, that suggested:

A) Todd thinks he's so cool.

B) Todd is going to die with some frozen balls.

And, apparently, one of those things was true.

Todd didn't want to see his dead body anymore. Not because it upset him. It just didn't interest him anymore. Like a plate of cold, half-eaten food on the table after dinner.

As the dog sunk its teeth into Todd's mitten, Todd pulled back, floated up and up until the trees became woods.

The park was busy now; people in brightly colored parkas getting out of cars, throwing sticks and yelling.

"GO GET IT!"

"GO GET IT, BOY!"

The people throwing stuff to their dogs sounded happy, Todd thought.

And then, a voice screamed out into the frosty winter morning, a cry for help, an old man's voice piercing the morning chill.

"HELP!!!"

The man yelling sounded like he was being throttled.

"OH MY GOD JESUS! SOMEONE CALL THE POLICE!"

The bright parkas stopped throwing balls and sticks and turned, converging toward the south end of the park. Through the pines, toward Todd.

A few minutes later, a black-and-white cop car came. Then an ambulance. Then more black-and-white cars.

More and more until the street was clogged with them.

By the time Todd floated back down to his body, there was a mass of people, mostly police officers, a woman with a plastic tackle box standing next to Todd's now very exposed body, pulling off a pair of plastic gloves.

Then a man and a woman, not in uniform, walked

through the crowd, which parted for them, if only slightly. It was a short white woman and a tall Black man, each carrying a cup of steaming coffee in nondescript Styrofoam cups. The woman had streaked blond hair tied up in a messy ponytail. She squatted down and looked at Todd's face. She had black eyeliner on all around her eyes, which made her look old. And like she wasn't very good at putting makeup on.

A strand of yellow hair fell in between her eyes as she snapped on a pair of lavender-colored rubber gloves.

The man sipped his coffee and pulled his gray cashmere knitted cap over his ears. He had tan leather gloves on.

The woman pursed her lips, covered in pink lipstick, and sniffed.

"Age?" the well-dressed man with the coffee asked.

She looked up and shook her head at the man. "Sixteen," she said. "Maybe seventeen?"

The male detective took another long sip of his coffee. He turned to the cop standing next to him, a rosy-faced man with two caps stacked under his police hat. "We know how long he's been here?"

"Not yet." The uniform wiped his nose with his sleeve. "Uh, sorry, I forgot your name."

"Detective Daniels," the well-dressed man said. "That's Detective Greevy over there. You new?"

They zipped Todd into a thick black bag, roughly the size of a body, and put him in the back of a van, like a piece of luggage.

Todd watched them drive to a gray building, unzip him, and put him on a table. Inside a room filled with metal tables, a big muscly guy with a mustache ran his hands over his face to wake himself up. Then he put his hands on the table next to Todd. "Right," he said.

Todd floated into the hallway, like in a dream, he thought. He floated up through the floor where the detectives sat in a medium-sized, windowless office.

Detective Greevy looked at her notebook and said, "Todd Mayer."

"Description fits." Daniels nodded. "His mom called him in missing last night. Riggs is at the house with her now. Single mom. No siblings."

"Fuck." Greevy patted her pockets distractedly. "Fuckity fuck."

Daniels leaned back in his chair, his long legs stretched under the desk and poked out the other side. "Davis and Riggs are bringing her in to identify the body."

Greevy laced her fingers together on her stomach, frowned. "A fucking kid."

Daniels nodded. "Fucking kid."

The fluorescent lights in the room made a clicking sound like hamster claws on glass. Greevy's chair squeaked as she turned it slightly to the left and right. "What about his clothes?" she asked.

Daniels shook his head. "No phone. No wallet. No clothes, although we found a pink mitten next to the body and someone's dog brought us the left one so we have the matching pair." He was looking at something on his computer. Clicking away. "There's a lot of foot traffic there in the morning. People walking their dogs. Maybe someone grabbed the other stuff. Uniforms are still searching."

Greevy stood up and wrote Todd's name on a whiteboard in black marker. It looked like *Todd Mager*.

She sat back down in her chair with a huff.

"Okay so . . ." Daniels looked around his desk. "I'll

get together the list of the local sex offenders? You'll geeet . . ."

Greevy stood and pulled the whiteboard toward her. "Phone records. Email. Social media. John'll look at his computer. We know what school he went to?"

"Albright Academy. Private school." Daniels looked at his computer. "You were right. Seventeen."

"Seventeen." Greevy sighed and walked out the door. Todd trailed after her, like a kite on a string. He followed Greevy outside, where she stood and smoked a cigarette in four long inhales, before stabbing it out on the metal railing, humming a song Todd didn't know.

A few minutes later, a cop arrived in Greevy and Daniels's office with a printed color photo of Todd and put it on the whiteboard, stuck with little bits of blue tape.

Todd remembered the day the photo was taken. It was in the grade-twelve commons. You had to sign up for a timeslot to get your photo taken. Todd picked lunch hour, when no one else would be there.

He remembered staring down the photographer, a sweaty man in a yellow button-down shirt that was too small and a little yellow stuffed chicken he was waving at the students as he took their photos.

"Smile?" the photographer offered.

Todd adjusted himself on the stool in front of the plastic backdrop with the school crest, which hung precariously behind him. "No," he said.

He straightened his spine, leveled his gaze, felt the stream of ice, very necessary ice, running through his veins.

Todd Mayer is cold as ice.

"Oh, come on," the photographer coaxed, shaking the chicken. "Just one smile."

And then the door behind the photographer opened.

And suddenly, a smile stretched across Todd's face. Like the smile was its own entity, pushing past Todd's practiced exterior of not caring about anything, like an energetic green sprout bursting up from the ground. Like the smile was a fugitive breaking free of Todd's mouth, forcing him to look like an asshole.

Because the boy who stepped inside the room at that moment was *the boy*, the boy with the mop of hair and the luggish smile, who plopped down in a chair pushed against the wall because his photo was next.

Before he could take the smile back, the photographer, who Todd imagined hated his job, snapped his picture.

A confluence of events that created the one and only photo of Todd as a young adult, grinning like an idiot.

It didn't even look like him.

And now that was the picture the detectives would see when they thought of Todd Mayer. That and the image of his dead body. What a dichotomy.

"All right," Greevy muttered, looking at the photo as she tapped the desk with her notebook, "let's do this."

GEORGIA
DEUX PERSONS *MANGING* THE *GOMME*

IT IS JANUARY 21ST, AND I am sitting in French class, next to Carrie, when I hear about Todd Mayer being dead.

We are "making verbs," as Madame De La Fontaine calls it. "Making verb sheets."

"*Kate manges un gommes avec*," Carrie says, writing on the group worksheet with a ballpoint that's running out of ink. Carrie's fingers are long and thin. Her nails are painted with clear polish she picks off when she's bored. She twirls her pen around her fingers, thinking. "*Avec* who?"

"How do you chew gum *together*?" I ask. The classroom smells like sour-cream-and-onion chips.

Carrie is super *blanche*. Super white. Let's say this is

possibly why Carrie used to be really popular, and I, being half Asian, have never been.

Which may or may not have something to do with being Asian, I'm not an expert on these things obviously.

Also Carrie is pretty loaded, or her family is, which, because this is an all-girls private school full of rich kids, is a thing. Also the white thing is a thing here.

Up until almost a year ago, Carrie was best friends with this girl Shirley Mason, who is the most popular person probably in our whole school, also super white, also rich. For most of the time I knew them, Carrie and Shirley had the same hair, same barrettes, same book bags. I think they used to take horseback-riding lessons together or something.

Then, suddenly, beginning of this school year, they stopped talking to each other. I have no idea why.

This September, when everyone was choosing their desks, instead of sitting next to Shirley and her crew, Carrie walked to the back of the classroom and stood behind the desk next to mine, which used to be the desk of a girl named Lena Hornbee.

Carrie pointed at the seat. Like I somehow had any say in the matter. I shrugged. Carrie sat down, careful like she wasn't sure the seat would hold. I sat down.

Then Carrie looked at me and pointed at the top of her head and said, "I like your piles."

By which I think she meant my two somewhat ear-shaped top buns I started wearing my hair in this year. Kind of an ode to a modern Princess Leia. Or not.

"Piles is something you get on your butt," I said. "It's like hemorrhoids."

Carrie didn't even widen her eyes. She just shrugged again. "Well then, I like your head hemorrhoids."

And that was it. Suddenly, Carrie Harper and I were friends.

(Meanwhile, for reasons seemingly only chair-related, Lena hangs out with Shirley and her crew now. That's how ridiculous life is.)

So now, months later, winter term, French class, leaning over her desk, which is next to mine, as all our desks are now, Carrie smiles a pea-sized smile. She has drawn two heads and draws puffy cheeks on them next to the text. "See? *Deux* persons manging the gum."

"That's just *deux* persons," I note. "How are they chewing *le gomme*?"

Carrie nods. "Right, right." She draws a big bubble coming out of one character's mouth and then draws a line into the other head's mouth. Carrie smiles. She has perfect teeth.

"See," she says, tapping her pen on the drawing.

"Okay, I see now," I say. *"Bon."*

Then Madame De La Fontaine walks in after being gone for, like, ten minutes (which is not strange, I'm pretty sure she goes behind the school to do *le smoking* while we do *le verbs*).

"Les filles," she says. She clears her throat. Madame De La Fontaine is one of the youngest teachers at St. Mildred's. She has long blond hair, and some days she wears jeans and an interesting T-shirt with a blazer, which feels kind of unteacherly to me. She looks like she should be talking to adults for a living. Maybe that's just a bias all the other teachers have created by wearing floral-printed polyester dresses and pantyhose all the time, like it's a rule.

I like Madame DLF because she almost never yells, which I appreciate.

Currently, she is twisting her wedding ring, turning it around her ring finger as she steps over to her desk. *"Les filles.* There is a subject, an incident, I know some of your classmates have been discussing *dans les messages texte* over lunch. And, it is very sad news, and the school has decided that we should make an announcement. So please put your pens and pencils, *tes stylos et tes crayon*, down, *s'il vous plaît*."

Carrie puts her pen down with a soft click.

Then someone behind me whispers, "Some kid was murdered."

Which Madame De La Fontaine doesn't hear. She puts her hands by her sides, like she's trying to stop messing with her ring, because it's not especially authoritative. "A boy. A boy from Albright, whom some of you might have known, has been found . . . dead. His name was . . . Todd Mayer."

. . .

Never heard of him.

Some girls in the classroom cover their mouths and look at each other. Some girls clearly feel better because they already knew some kid got murdered. One girl looks like she's going to throw up. Another girl on the other side of me gasps, "Oh my God!"

"Oh my GOD!"

It is impossible to say if any of these girls actually knew Todd or are just being dramatic because the girls at this school are kind of prone to dramatics. Like when we had an earthquake and three people went home with anxiety.

It was like a .0004 or something. Like a ground fart. Someone else passed out and had to be taken to the hospital.

You want to say this means girls are softies, but these same girls crush bone on the field hockey team so clearly it's complicated.

Madame De La Fontaine tells us this is a tragedy and if anyone would like to go to the nurse's office, they can.

Two girls, the usual suspects including Lena, immediately raise their hands.

"That's my brother's school," I say, later, after not doing anything for the rest of French, and not doing a ton of work or paying attention for the rest of the school day. "What grade was he in?"

Carrie digs in her pockets for what she's always digging in her pockets for, gum. "Twelfth, I think."

"That's Mark's grade," I say.

Carrie raises her eyebrows. "Oh yeah, your brother goes to Albright."

After school, we go to the food truck with the weird painting of the old man made out of French fries on the side, and we buy a floater of fries to share. The French fry guy looks like someone who would rape you if he found you alone in an alley. That's what I've decided anyway, because I watch a lot of *Law & Order Special Victims Unit*, a show where someone died once by having a banana shoved up their butt (which is obviously deadly). Fry Guy has long white hair that sprouts out of his head in the same arc as a fern's leaves and a mustache that any normal person would shave off because it looks like an old rug stuck to his face, like a mustache a disinterested five-year-old would draw on a face. And it makes him look, as I said, like a felon.

In my humble opinion.

But his fries are three dollars for a small. So I'm willing to overlook that stuff.

Carrie is skinny and can basically eat anything and it will never affect her body size. Carrie said her mom was the same way when she was younger but now her mom is huge.

"Like a walrus who only wears boots," Carrie says, eating a fry with a tiny wooden fork. "So when I'm twenty, I'm going to have to decide if I want to stop eating this crap or be a walrus."

"I think walruses are cool," I say. "Sturdy. Reliable."

"Not ALL walruses," Carrie adds. "It's like . . . not all beavers."

"Sure. Obviously not ALL walruses are cool." I concur, popping a fry in my mouth, open-mouth chewing so the cold air keeps my mouth from burning.

It's freezing out but if we walk and eat fries it's not too bad. The grease works its way into your veins and warms your blood.

I hold my fry on my fork in the cold air and watch the steam rise up from the potato horizon.

"So a kid is dead," I say, shoving the fry in my mouth and chewing. "That's fucked up."

Carrie chews, steam huffing out of her mouth and into the air. "It's fucked up to be murdered."

"Was he *murdered*?" I stop walking.

"If he died of cancer, they wouldn't say 'found dead,'" Carrie notes, speedwalking.

"True," I say, jogging to catch up. "Maybe a pervert did it."

"Sure." Carrie shrugs.

I'm thinking of saying that maybe it was the French fry guy but it feels too soon.

Carrie tosses the empty cardboard tray into the trash

and pulls out a wrapped stick from one of her many gum stashes.

We round the corner and, with the motor skills and speed of a practiced pickpocket, Carrie pops three pieces of gum from three different packs into her mouth. I shove my hands into my pockets. The air is getting colder with every step. It's like someone's watching us walk and turning down the lights and turning off the heat the closer we get to being in between warm school and warm home. It's so weird that it gets dark so soon after school. I know it's the season, but it still feels unfair.

Most of the girls at our school our age have cars, presumably warm cars, and several rip past us, tearing through the layer of slush on the street. Shirley Mason drives a select group of girls home every day, blasting music and singing with her pack. Shirley Mason has a new SUV. Why does someone who is sixteen need a new SUV?

To me, it suggests a general disinterest in being anything useful in the world. But that's just me.

I wonder if it's, like, triggering for Carrie to see these SUVs full of rich girls who used to be her friends.

I also wonder why Carrie, whose parents are loaded, doesn't have an SUV.

I pull my mittens out of my pocket and push my greasy fingers inside. It's weird how mittens are cold when you first put them on. Mittens need you to warm them up.

We walk in silence for a bit. Carrie doesn't wear boots, ever. Not even if it's raining. Her school oxfords are so worn they're not even black anymore, they're the color of a really old cat, like when the fur wears away and you can see the little bits of cat skin.

I wear boots outside because I don't like cold feet. My boots make me sound like I'm dragging myself across the sidewalk. It's a creepy sound.

Scuff. Scuff. Scuff. Scuff.

My boots are my brother Mark's old boots, which I got hand-me-down year because he got this part-time job shoveling walks so he had to get fancy new boots that are like the SUV of boots. Mark's old boots are big, but I kind of like them being too big. I feel like a robot in them. A winter robot. With warm feet.

At her bus stop, Carrie stops and tilts her head at me.

Then she says, "Hey, remember in French class? How two people can't eat gum?"

"Yeah?"

There's a woman at the bus stop with a tiny poodle

in a knapsack perfectly sized for a tiny dog. The poodle's head is sticking out like a doll.

This is what I'm thinking about when I feel cold, wet, sticky fingers on my lips. And I taste orange and mint. A mix of what I'm guessing is Dentyne Ice and Bubblicious Orange. And something else.

I'm chewing Carrie's gum.

It's a thing that affects my whole body. Like my whole body is now focused on what is happening in my mouth. On what just happened. That is 100 percent who I am for three seconds.

I look over at Carrie, who is licking the residue off her fingers, not even an eyebrow raised. NOTHING. She turns and steps into the bus. "Later."

"Later." My lips are sticky. And vibrating.

I don't watch Carrie's bus pull away. I divert some of my body's resources from my gum-filled mouth to my legs and walk home. I walk so fast my heart pounds in my chest like a gorilla.

How can two people chew gum?

Snow is falling. White flakes float into my eyes and stick to my lashes like squirrels on a fence.

My face buzzes, even more every time I bite down into Carrie's gum.

I walk home feeling like one of those bobblehead dolls with the big head on a spring. By the time I get to my house, I've chewed Carrie's gum a hundred times.

Dentyne Ice, Bubblicious and . . . Juicy Fruit?

Todd Mayer is dead, I think, chewing. Murdered.

The only information I have about murder is from TV, which is that people tend to be murdered by people they know. Often husbands. Angry husbands. Or vengeful wives (which my mom has pointed out is inaccurate). I'm pretty sure Todd had neither.

Still, as someone who's spent seven years in an all-girls private school, a school where, in grade six, Shirley Mason renamed me Garbagia, a name that stuck for three years, I can see that proximity could up your chances of wanting to kill someone, if that some-one was an asshole. Consistently.

I get home as the winter sky goes from gray to black, Carrie's gum like a penny on my tongue.

Mark is standing in the kitchen when I get inside, layered up in his arctic winter coat that makes him look even bigger than he is, and he is a wall of muscle. His hair is all sticking up in his man ponytail he puts his hair in when he's at home (but he always takes the elastic out before he walks out the door).

"Hey, G," he says, a half a banana in his mouth.

"Hey, Mark," I say, shaking off my coat as the heat of the house hits me like a tidal wave.

My mom keeps the house at a balmy seventy-five degrees at all times, and she's super into "bundling up." Neither my brother nor I has ever owned a winter item of clothing that's less than six inches thick, a layer of down between us and what I would say are not necessarily arctic temperatures.

As a result, I feel like it's possible that I will never truly understand cold or winter.

"Holy cow." I lightly kick at Mark's bear-sized gym bag with the toe of my boot. "This thing is HUGE! It looks like you have a body in there."

"Quit it." Mark flips the garbage bin open and tosses in his peel. "You're getting salt shit all over it."

With our matching big boots, we make twin *Scuff Scuff Scuff* (me) *Scoot Scoot Scoot* (Mark) noises as Mark grabs another banana and I grab crackers from the cupboard. My mom would kick our asses if she saw us in our boots in the house.

"Don't you wrestle in your underwear? What do you need a huge bag of shit for?"

Mark grabs another banana and shoves the whole

thing in his mouth in a way that is both fascinating and gross. From what I've seen of Mark eating, and granted it's a limited study but still, it is truly amazing that teenage boys don't die from choking on food every day.

Mark frowns because I'm staring at him. "It's just stuff I need. I got a lot of stuff. That okay with you?"

I wince at the view of banana-pulp-in-mouth. "I guess."

Mark never asks me how school was. Or any other kind of small talk. I also never ask Mark how his school is, but I assume it's fine because I'm pretty sure Mark does not have to deal with people giving him crappy nicknames because he's a big boy jock who looks like he could pound you into the earth with his pinky.

Mark grabs yet another banana from the seemingly endless supply in our tropical temperature house and stuffs it in his pocket.

"You're like ninety percent banana," I say. "Who knew the key to muscle was banana?"

"Yeah, well, you're ninety percent carbohydrates."

"Yes, I am."

Mark hoists up his bag, mouth full. "Tell mom I'm at Trevor's."

"'Kay."

Scoot. Scoot. Scoot.

When I was younger, I wished Mark and I went to the same school so he could help make me cool, but now I'm pretty sure that's not how it works. Now I think it would have possibly been worse because he has too much dirt on me.

"You've seen me in a bonnet," I told him once. "I don't know if I should allow you to live."

"Like I give a shit that you wore a bonnet," he said, as he effortlessly shoved me into the couch so hard it knocked the wind out of me. "You also used to shit your pants."

"Everyone shits their pants," I yelled back. "You probably shit your pants, too. I just wasn't alive to see it."

"Yeah so," Mark frowned. "Whatever."

"You're a genius."

"You're a bonnet wearer."

Scoot. Scoot. Scoot.

"BYE!" I scream, from the kitchen.

"LATER!" Mark screams back from the front hall.

Scoot. Scoot. Scoot.

The door slams before I can ask Mark about Todd.

TODD
WHAT DO YOU KNOW ABOUT TODD MAYER?

ALBRIGHT ACADEMY, AN ALL-BOYS PRIVATE school, looked like a private school from a movie, vaguely British, Todd had always thought, bricks and ivy on the outside and pristine marble, polished wood, and brass on the inside.

In the hall, three steps in from the front door, a huge crest was embedded in the black-and-white marble floor, the Albright crest: a shield with an eagle holding a sprig of something in one claw and a bar of gold in the other.

Todd always thought the bird looked like Scrooge McDuck's evil eagle brother.

The main feature of the crest was the taboo against stepping on it.

Daniels and Greevy didn't know about this taboo. Greevy stood, that morning, her salty snow-soaked detective shoes on the eagle's beak, looking at the fili-gree and muttering, "The fuck."

Greevy was wearing her leather coat, a button-down gray shirt, and black pants. Her hair still tied up but falling out of the elastic like she'd slept in her ponytail.

Daniels had a long wool coat on, a cashmere scarf that was just a shade darker than his coat. All char-coal wool underneath.

Greevy looked like a cop. Daniels looked like a lawyer.

When Todd first arrived at Albright, he was assigned a senior to show him the ropes. Every freshman got one. Todd's was Doug Harper. Doug Harper, third gen-eration Albright boy, had a face that looked like pizza dough and more red hair than Todd had ever seen on a human. Probably a full body of Irish setter red fur under his white button-down and gray slacks, not that Todd was picturing it or anything.

Doug Harper was not all that thrilled to be show-ing a scrawny freshman the ropes, even though, con-ceivably, it was his birthright.

Doug Harper told Todd that the hallway was

haunted by a dead caretaker. If you stand on the crest, Doug told him, the ghost of the dead caretaker will follow you home and kill you in your sleep.

"He likes little pussy boys like you," Doug sneered at Todd, as they stood in the hallway, next to the crest. "He's gonna ram his broom handle up your ass."

After he said it, Doug shoved Todd forward and tried to get him to fall on the crest. But Todd was catlike and he threw his body to the side, falling to the ground just shy of the crest.

Doug Harper graduated three years ago. But of course there were a hundred other Doug Harpers to take his place.

A clip-clop of little feet echoed through the hallway.

"Here he comes," Greevy muttered, looking up. "Geez, guy LOOKS like a principal."

Principal Spot moved across the floor in a series of tiny, crisp, quick steps that matched his little bald head and tiny face. His brown suit looked like it was made in a store that makes clothes for tiny principals. Spot stopped just short of the crest, like a diver lining up his toes to the edge of the diving board.

"Detectives," he said, extending a little pink hand. "I am Principal Spot. Welcome to Albright Academy."

Greevy shook his hand first. "Thank you," she said.

Spot patted the brown folder in his left hand. "This is the complete record of Todd Mayer's time in our school," he said. "He was a longtime student, as perhaps you know. Of course if you have any questions, I am happy to be of any service."

Spot looked up at the ceiling. "Obviously his death has come as an incredible shock." He sighed. "A great loss for the whole school."

Greevy took her notebook out of her pocket and tapped it in her palm. "We'd like to speak to all the students in his grade, today, and all the teaching staff who had him as a student," she said. "And anyone else you think he was close to. Sports connections and clubs and so on."

Spot nodded vigorously. "Certainly. I will be escorting you. We have four grade-twelve homerooms."

Sweat ran down the side of Spot's face and pooled in the divot between his neck and his once-crisp white collar.

Todd often wondered, when he saw Principal Spot mincing through the hallways, why someone like Spot became a principal. Because you could see in Spot, presumably even if you weren't someone with

Todd's life experience, that he was someone people made fun of. Probably high school was hell for young Spot. He was an easy person to imitate, and many at Albright did a solid Principal Spot impersonation (though not Todd).

Why walk back into the fire? Revenge?

Greevy held her arm out. "After you," she said.

It was 10:00 a.m., forty minutes into first period. The halls were empty. Spot walked fast. The sound of Greevy's shoes echoed as she stomped down the empty hallway. Wood floors and white walls. The pictures of graduating students of 1993, 1994, 1995, 1996, faces so similar they blurred together like the dotted line down the middle of a highway.

Possibly the only time any of those boys could be considered inert, Todd had always thought, was when their confident smiles were behind glass.

Principal Spot veered left, past the same-smiles of the classes of 2001, 2002, and 2003, knocked on room 214, and opened the door. Homeroom 12C.

Todd's homeroom.

Todd's OLD homeroom.

Being a ghost takes getting used to.

As Spot and Daniels and Greevy entered the room,

the sound of voices inside the classroom stopped dead. At the front of the class, Mr. Devoe looked up and stopped writing on the board. Twenty-four boys turned and watched as Greevy walked up to the teacher's desk at the front of the class. Spot followed a few steps behind her.

It occurred to Todd that, if you didn't know their names, know who only ate cheese for lunch, know who once shit himself in gym, who didn't wear socks even though it's part of the uniform and a sign of basic human decency, it was just twenty-four boys. Twenty-four boys, sitting silent in their perfectly straight rows of desks. A perfect square (minus one) of boys in uniform: dress shirts and pants, blue and gray striped ties, groomed heads and white shirts, sweaty faces. They looked at one another without moving, eyes clicking left and right.

Greevy cleared her throat. Daniels crossed his arms and leaned on the wall at the back of the classroom.

"Hey so, okay, so I'm Detective Greevy," Greevy said as she sat half her butt on the corner of the teacher's desk. "I'm here today with Detective Daniels; that's him back there. I'm sure your teachers have told you by now that your fellow student Todd Mayer's death is being investigated by police. Which means that we are trying to find out some more about what happened to him the night he died."

It was so fucking quiet you could hear each individual blink, the soft sound of each breath. Everyone in the room picked a spot that wasn't Greevy and focused on it.

Greevy adjusted herself on the desk. Waited.

A chair scooted and made a loud squeak. It was the kid who shit himself in gym class two years ago. A kid Todd often used as a touchstone to remember that horrible things happened to other people at Albright.

Greevy waited some more.

The kid who only ate cheese coughed.

Their ties were all tight around their necks today. Did someone spread the word that detectives were coming, Todd wondered. Or were they always this still?

Greevy looked out over the sea of faces. "The last information we have about Todd is that he left his house on the evening of Tuesday, January twentieth. Two nights ago. I want to talk to anyone who knows where he might have been going that night, anyone who heard from him or saw him that night. Or talked to him that day. Is there anything you know about what might have been going on with him? Something hard to talk about maybe?"

As if she'd pulled a string, bodies started moving. Boys turned their heads, looking, waiting for someone to say something. But no one did. Shoulders went up and heads went down.

Someone was bouncing his knee under his desk. Todd looked at him.

"Looks like you're going to die with some frooozen balls, homo!"

Daniels pushed off the wall at the back of the class, walked up the aisle of desks. Crossing the invisible line between visitor and student. Invading their space. "I want you to really think, now. Did Todd say anything to anyone that seems like something we should know? Maybe it's something that might not seem important, something small?"

Silence.

Daniels stopped in between desks. "You know, this is not a big school," he said. "Just because you weren't friends with him, doesn't mean you didn't hear something about what was going on with his life. And whatever you know is going to help us find out who hurt him. Anything out of the ordinary.

Anything going on that could have involved Todd. Anything."

A bunch of boys looked down. Shook their heads.

Greevy folded her arms over her chest. "This is not about getting in trouble or getting someone else in trouble. This is about a student at your school who has died. Right? Wouldn't you want someone to speak up for you? Give your parents some peace of mind?"

Parent.

Earlier that morning, the detectives had stopped in to see Todd's mother.

She met them at the door wearing a long, droopy sweater that she would normally never wear. Inside, the house was quiet except for the sound of his mother's sisters, Lucy and Laura, who were huddled in the long, yellow-tiled kitchen, making coffee, putting things in cupboards, listening.

Despite the fact that, as a ghost, Todd took up no space at all, the house seemed suddenly small. Or crowded. Maybe it was watching Greevy and Daniels squeeze through the narrow hallways lined with his mother's bookcases full of romance novels and the old encyclopedias she collected. Maybe it was the way Daniels eventually perched on the faded purple loveseat in the living room, while Greevy took the chair by the window with the wool throw draped over the back.

This mix of things that used to populate his life, a crowd of objects that only went together because his mother put them all in the same room.

Todd wondered if the detectives were looking and deciding that this mix of stuff meant they knew something about Todd, while his mother offered them coffee. As she sat on the green couch with the pink flowers and the hole in the left cushion they covered with a throw pillow and told the detectives about the last time she saw Todd.

She told the detectives that Todd left the house that night at 8:30 p.m. She said that Todd told her he was going to see a movie at the Revue Cinema, at 9:00 p.m. Which is something Todd did a lot, the movie thing, by himself. He liked old movies, and the Revue. Eighties classics for $5. All-night Swedish film festivals for $4.

Ferris Bueller. Rear Window. Planet of the Apes. Dear Wendy.

Just Todd and a bunch of men in superhero T-shirts, quietly munching and watching. The smell of soap and popcorn. It was relaxing.

That night, Todd told his mother the movie ended at 11:00 p.m. Todd was supposed to be home at 11:30 p.m. If he caught the bus right after the movie, he could be home in twenty minutes. Thirty max.

At midnight, Todd's mother called his cell phone and there was no answer. She called twelve times after that. Which was significant because very, very few people called Todd on his phone.

When Todd's mother stopped talking, Daniels leaned over from his perch and said, "I know this is incredibly difficult, Mrs. Mayer. I know this is the worst thing that can happen to a person."

Todd's mother whispered that she hadn't slept. It was a throaty whisper. Todd's ghost felt it; it vibrated his nonexistent body like a bow sliding over a violin string, like the feeling when you run the pad of your finger over concrete. It was a strange sensation because it was the only sensation Todd's ghost has felt since he stopped feeling anything.

Todd's Aunt Lucy scampered into the living room from the kitchen and took Todd's mother's hand. Todd's Aunt Lucy was the one paying for private school, because she worked in real estate instead of having kids. She used to call Todd "The Brain" and ask him about girlfriends. Todd's Aunt Laura, who Todd didn't like because she was kind of rude to his mom, he thought, came in with a plate of cookies no one ate.

Daniels looked up at the photo of Todd's father, who died when Todd was five. It was a picture from a summer vacation when Todd was just a baby, one of those flared out sunny photos where you can't really see anyone's faces.

"He told me," Todd's mother said, softly, to the little china cat on the coffee table, "he told me he would be home right after the movie. He said he had studying to do."

"He studied that late?" Daniels asked. "Good student, huh?"

"He was a good kid." Todd's mother's voice was barely a whisper. "I called him the homework machine. He wanted to go to a good college. He wanted good grades."

Todd's mother fell into a sob, into the ample side of Aunt Lucy, who wrapped her arm around her.

Todd watched as Greevy and Daniels carefully set their coffee cups on their coasters, already inching back and away before Aunt Lucy stood and asked them if there was anything else they needed.

Not at the moment, they said. And they thanked her for her time. Again. And gave their condolences, again.

At the school, Daniels and Greevy went to all four homerooms, the same routine every time.

After each speech, Greevy handed a stack of her cards to every teacher.

"If you think of anything, anything, even if you don't think it's relevant, I want you to call us," she told every class, holding up a card to show them she was leaving them behind. "This is how we find out what happened to Todd. We need your help."

Every teacher in every homeroom took the cards and told Daniels that Todd was an incredibly gifted student.

Afterwards, Daniels and Greevy went to the principal's office. Spot had run out to talk to a parent. Parents had been calling the school all day, Spot said, because there was a lot of misinformation going around. One parent thought Todd died on the school grounds. Because the news headlines said, "Boy Found Dead," but it didn't say where.

Daniels sat on the brown leather couch in Spot's office. Greevy stood and stared at Spot's desk.

It was one of those desks with a leather blotter built into the top. There was laptop and a picture in the far corner. She picked up the frame. It was photo of Spot and his dog.

"What do you think the dog's name is?" She smirked.

"Doug." Daniels flipped open Todd's file on his lap. "So. No friends," he said, scanning the papers inside.

"Apparently not." Greevy frowned.

"Or scared friends," Daniels said. "Nervous friends."

"Possibly."

"Enemies?" Daniels asked, turning a page. "Do seventeen-year-olds have enemies?"

"Sure." Greevy's voice landed like a hammer on metal.

Todd's file was slim. It contained: a printed list of grades, a list of Todd's extracurricular activities (one), a list of honors and awards, medical history. A few forms Todd's mom signed for field trips: science center, aquarium, planetarium, museum of earth sciences.

"Badminton team," Daniels noted, with what Todd decided to hear as respect.

Greevy sounded incredulous. "Badminton? Nice fucking school. Badminton team."

Todd thought that was generous. He played three games before he found out what the badminton equipment was called: a cock. Technically a "shuttlecock," but a cock nonetheless.

By grade ten, Todd knew better than to leave any openings, any vulnerabilities. So he quit the team.

"So Todd Mayer had no friends; he played badminton and got good grades." Greevy sighed, pulling books out of Spot's shelf and inspecting the titles.

"And he was in the Social Sciences Tutoring League." Daniels looked at Greevy, eyebrow raised.

"They call it a fucking LEAGUE?"

Spot returned, even sweatier, and dropped behind his desk like a small bag of potatoes. "I hope your visits to the homerooms went well," he said, brushing invisible crumbs off his desk.

"We didn't get a lot from the students today," Greevy answered. "But we'll be back."

Spot nodded vigorously. "Of course. Anything we can do. With parental consent where appropriate of course."

"Can you tell me about the social studies tutoring program?" Daniels pointed at the file.

"Yes." Spot planted his hands firmly on his desk. "It

was a program started this year by Mr. McVeeter. It was intended as a way to get students to use peer support in improving their grades. Obviously, a great learning opportunity on both sides. We're trying to move to more peer support programs, which was a challenge we put to our faculty last year. Colleges like them as an extracurricular, and it helps alleviate some of the pressure on the teaching staff."

Spot paused and looked at Daniels and Greevy. Like he was suddenly unsure as to what he was supposed to be saying. Spot turned to his computer. "I can get you a list of the other students in the program if you like."

"We'd like." Greevy smiled. She was looking at his computer. "Is Mr. McVeeter, league director, in today? We'd like to speak to him as well."

"Ah." Spot looked up from his screen. "I'm afraid Mr. McVeeter called in sick this morning. Food poisoning. Some sort of chicken, I believe."

Greevy scratched the name into her notebook. It looked like *Mr. McVeeper* in her scrawled handwriting.

Daniels pulled another piece of paper out of the file, a small square pink slip. "There's an incident report in here," he said. "Can you tell us about that?"

Todd had never actually seen an incident report in

the flesh, although it was something he'd heard teachers threaten students with. It looked like one of the memos his mother used to keep around the house to write messages on.

Spot stopped typing. "That was before my time," he said. "That would have been during the previous principal's run, Principal Tek—"

Daniels cut in. "Would there be something you could pull up in your files? Since you weren't present?"

Daniels stood and placed the pink slip on Spot's desk.

Spot pulled it over with his little finger. "We are still implementing the online records so we don't have everything up. But I will see if I can find some more information."

Seconds later, Spot handed a printed page to Greevy. "The names of the students in the tutoring league. It appears there was only one tutor, which was Todd. Looks like there were only four being tutored: Chris Mattieu, Devon Marcus, Cameron Hill, and Mark Walker."

"Small," Greevy said.

"Pilot program," Spot corrected, crisply. "I'm sure most of our students were doing fairly well in the humanities, with the exception of a handful, who were struggling. Mr. McVeeter is a very successful educator. We have a dedicated teaching staff here at Albright, as I'm sure you've heard."

Daniels nodded. "I'm sure you do. We'd like to talk to all four boys."

"Yes. It is Friday so our students who are team members might already have left." Spot typed something else into his computer. "Yes, I'm afraid two of them have just left for a swim meet so they are no longer on campus. Do you want to talk to the other boys?"

Greevy and Daniels exchanged neutral looks.

"We'll come back," Daniels said. "Talk to them all together."

Spot nodded. "In the meantime, anything you need . . ." He looked like he had to go to the bathroom, like he was holding it in or had been for hours. Days. "We can inform parents . . . I'm sorry, what should we inform our school parents?"

"You can tell them an investigation is underway and we are looking for information from students on Todd Mayer's whereabouts on the night he disappeared," Greevy said.

Later, in the car, Greevy lit a smoke and breathed a long sigh. It was cold and Daniels had the heat blasting as he rubbed his hands together. "You got one smoke and then that's it. You're killing me with that shit, Greevy."

Greevy shook her head. "I feel like I've been staring at a brick wall of teenage boys all day."

"Really fucking quiet teenage boys," Daniels agreed. "With nothing to say about a kid they probably went to school with for years."

"Yup." Greevy exhaled a plume of smoke out the window.

"I'm putting my money on 'Incident Report,'" Daniels said, pulling out of the lot.

Todd was a ghost and no longer had any money to bet.

Todd drifted out the window with the smoke of Greevy's cigarette, up into the now gray sky. He was already getting used to being so much less than he was when he was alive. Maybe because there's something in death that makes being nothing feel natural. Maybe because he had somehow always been a sort of figment. A slim file.

A slim file at a school like Albright was his accomplishment. Of course, he hadn't considered that would make his murder investigation more difficult.

You don't think about death, like that, when you're alive. You think about surviving. And Todd was sure that everything he had done, everything he was, was helping him survive high school.

Except for that one thing. One mistake.

The last night of his life, when he walked out of his front door at 8:00 p.m.

Todd tried to remember what his mother looked like, tucking into the couch with her bag of pistachios to watch her favorite show about small-town crime.

"It's freezing," she said. "Take your mittens."

Todd walked out the front door. At the end of the stone walk, he stopped. He knew his mom watched him from the window. It was snowing lightly. Todd held up his pink mittens for her to see. Mittens he made himself, which he kept hidden in his coat pockets when he was at school. Then he turned left and walked down the sidewalk toward the bus stop.

The Revue isn't open on Tuesday. Which Todd's mom didn't know.

There was something about that night. Maybe he was just nervous. Todd remembered the feeling in his stomach, loose and cold like the snow.

That night it was colder than Todd thought it would

be, air like a thousand knives. Todd remembered breathing in deeply, sucking as much cold air into his lungs as he could, filling himself with it, like splashing cold water on his face, bracing.

Just relax, okay?

Greevy turned on the radio. Led Zeppelin. Daniels rolled his eyes. "First cigarettes now this. You got ten minutes of this shit before I change it."

Greevy bit her lip. "You think something's going to come up, and it's some random guy in the park? Cute kid like that? Alone at night? Looking for company?"

"Cute?" Daniels raised an eyebrow.

Cute was never how Todd saw himself, but then you learn a lot about yourself when you're dead. When it's clearly too late to do anything about it.

"You know," Greevy grumbled, "young."

Daniels paused at the stoplight.

Greevy tossed her smoke out the window. "*Do* you think it's some random guy in the park?"

"No," Daniels said, and he gunned the car through the slush of snow. "I don't."

GEORGIA
WHERE WERE YOU
THAT NIGHT?

TODAY, AFTER SCHOOL, CARRIE IS leaning against my locker. She's holding her knapsack, which is black leather and scuffed in a fashionable way, in her hand. Holding it the way she holds all her expensive things, like she gets it but she doesn't care. Her pearl gray scarf, which matches her, I imagine, very expensive pearl gray wool coat, is double looped around her neck.

When I tie a scarf around my neck, I look like I'm being strangled. I don't know why.

As she's walking up to my locker, I check my face for any stray weird stuff because that sort of thing happens to ME.

"Hey," Carrie says, "It's Friday. School's out. Got any big plans?"

"Um," I say. "No?"

"How about coffee?"

I shove the many bags of popcorn, my school eating vice, into my locker so they don't spill out onto the floor and grab my giant puffy purple coat, which smells like popcorn, and click my locker door shut. "Sure."

So we get coffees, then go to the park where Todd Mayer's body was found.

Which is my contribution to the afternoon's activities.

I have been thinking about Todd since I found out he died. I also watched three hours of *CSI* last night, and I want to see the park.

I also overheard three girls in bio talking about how they can't go to the park now because of Todd.

At the time I was all, "The girls at my school are really really not smart."

Now that I'm here, it feels both weirdly important to be here and kind of like some high school girl thing where you do something because you want to do something significant and then you realize WHY something is significant.

Because someone DIED here.

The sun is going down. Or it's down already. It's

hard to tell because the sky is so gray and the gray is everywhere, like an eraser, like a pervasive non-thing.

The lightest thing is the ground, which is one smooth, even dome of crisp white snow, with the trees down at the bottom of the hill poking out like thick black hairs.

"I heard the lady who this park is named after used to bring her dogs here to poop because she didn't want them to poop in her fancy backyard," I say, the snow crunching under my boots. I can't remember where I heard that. Did Mark tell me that?

"Really? I heard she was an activist," Carrie says, looking at her coffee cup.

"Maybe she's both."

The dog walkers are gone. Or missing. You can just see some little footprints, like the little holes left in cupcakes after you pull off all the sprinkles. I wonder if maybe the dog walkers are also too creeped out to come here at night now that someone died here. Maybe they're keeping the dogs away so they won't mess with evidence.

Carrie takes long sips of her coffee and stares out into the dark.

I am actually not a big fan of coffee, and mostly I drink it because it's something Carrie likes to do, so I let the thick black liquid graze my lip before I let it slide back through its little hole and back into my cup. It tastes like tar.

There's a sound. Flapping. Like a thousand flags. I step forward to see the bit of yellow police tape shifting in the trees.

"I feel like a cop," I say, in my exaggerated serious cop voice, breaking the silence with a sort of joke because I'm cool.

"Yeah? Because of the coffee or because we're next to a crime scene?" Carrie asks, not yes-and-ing.

"Both," I say, now equally serious. "Would you know what to look for, in a crime scene?"

"I think they teach you that in cop school," Carrie says.

"I think it's instinct," I say, with the authority of someone who watches a lot of TV. "It's like a Where's Waldo type of thing, where you have to be able to see the little out-of-place details. Have a soft eye."

"Like what," Carrie asks.

"You have to ask yourself, 'What doesn't belong?'" I say, turning my coffee cup around in my hand. "The out-of-place thing."

"Don't killers think about that stuff?" Carrie asks. "If I were a killer, I'd think of that stuff."

"It could be a skin cell," I add. "Hard to know you've left behind a skin cell."

"You could wear gloves," Carrie says. "That would stop skin-cell leakage."

"Criminals always leave a thread," I assure her. "Or a little piece of plastic or a footprint or a hair. You could leave a piece of the glove; that's a clue, too. Or a piece of twine or—"

"Something small," Carrie says, running her finger over the lid of her coffee. "I get it."

It feels like we're standing in a painting. It feels surreal, if I think about it, which I am. I'm actually not really feeling sad. Because I didn't know Todd. I did see a photo of him on the news. He looked like a goof with big zits and a big ridiculous smile on his face.

No judgment obviously. Since he's dead. School photos suck obviously.

"Let's go," Carrie says, swiveling. "It's freezing."

I am walking behind Carrie, watching the edge of her shoes crack the thin sheet of snow on top of the grass, thinking a few things, as I often do.

My mom once wrote a book about a girl who doesn't have any friends. It's called *Come Play with Molly!*

Come Play with Molly! is about a little girl, Molly,

who wishes and wishes for friends, and then one day she wakes up and her backyard is full of little boys and girls, ready to play with her.

I shit you not, that is the story.

Needless to say, *Come Play with Molly!* sucks.

First of all because I know my own friendless childhood was the inspiration and second because the ending is total bullshit.

My mom doesn't remember actual shit about what it means to be a kid.

If she did, the book would just be called *Molly Has No Friends but She's Dealing with It.*

Or:

Molly Had No Friends So She Is WARY of Friends Who Just Show Up All of the Sudden and Act Like They Are Her Friends.

I look at Carrie, who looks pretty fucking cold. I search for my mittens in my pockets.

Carrie's bare hands are both curled around her coffee cup. Her fingers are thin like icicles.

"Do you have an alibi for that night?" I ask, in my TV cop voice.

Carrie snorts. "Uh. I was home watching TV."

"Yeah sure, me too." I nod.

"Oh yeah?" Carrie raises an eyebrow. "What were you watching?"

"The Food Network."

Carrie scoffs. "The FOOD NETWORK. Right."

"It was a special about birthday cakes, where these three teams had to make a birthday cake with a car theme," I say. "Also I watched a BBC thing about a town where everyone hates one another but won't talk about it."

I toss my coffee, still full, into the garbage can. It hits the bottom with a tell-tale THUD. "You think Todd Mayer knew his killer?"

Carrie stares up at the snow swirling in the street-lights. "How would I know?"

Sometimes, when Carrie talks, I hear Shirley's voice. That tinny, quick disdain that haunted my life from 8:30 a.m. to 3:30 p.m. from grade five until relatively recently.

Shirley Thinks You're a Waste of Space. A nonexistent and possibly too real title for a children's book.

At the edge of the park, Carrie looks at me with what feels like some sort of piercing, mind-reading stare.

"We should have said something," she says. "We should have said something nice, for Todd."

"Yeah," I say, "like RIP or something."

Carrie steps forward and grabs my arm, digging her fingers into the puff of my coat. "Rest in peace, Todd."

She holds my arm for another second, then let's go.

"Cool," I say, because I can't think of anything else.

We walk the rest of the way to Carrie's bus stop in silence.

At the stop, Carrie turns her head to the side, exhales a long stream of warm air, like a person smoking a cigarette, turning their head to blow out a stream of smoke. I can see it curling into the cold night, like milk in coffee. A little bit of Carrie mixing into the night.

There's a sharp squeal of brakes as the bus slides into the mush of snow by the sidewalk.

"Anyway," I say, "I'll see you Monday, obviously."

Carrie shoves her hands into her pockets and turns toward the bus. "Sure," she says, and jumps up onto the step, not looking back.

When I get home, there's a car in the driveway. A big gray SUV with the motor running. Mark's best friend, Trevor Bathurst, destroying the environment. I can see him in the driver's seat, looking at his phone.

I've only said like three sentences to him, but I strongly suspect that Trevor is the sort of person who is a dick.

"HELLO!" I yell as I throw open the front door.

Mark and my mom are standing by the counter in the kitchen. My mom has the big pot out, and I can hear a loud sizzling noise. The kitchen smells like watery beans and tomato. Normally it's my dad who makes chili, the typical dad dinner where a dad makes a dinner that seems like it's this big effort but really it's no bigs because it's all he does other than light the barbeque in the summer.

Because he's a lawyer and not a cook, he says.

My mom calls out my dad on this stuff all the time.

"Well, I'm an artist and not a maid," she says.

Right. We get it. You both have jobs. We all have things to do. Why are you telling me this?

Mark and my mom both stop talking when I walk in the kitchen and drop my bag. Like I've clearly interrupted something. Mark is pulling on his coat.

"Hello to you, too," I say.

"Hey, G," Mark says.

"Hey. What's going on?"

"Nothing." Mark grabs a banana from the basket on the counter. "I'll be back for dinner," he says, backing toward the door.

I am suddenly starving, though not for any of

Mark's ridiculously healthy snacks. Like. Fruit? No, thank you.

Mark hikes his bag up higher on his shoulder. "Uh. You good?"

"Yeah. Just hungry."

"Cool."

I look in the pot. It's still a big chili iceberg with chili water sizzling up steam. My mom stabs it with a spoon as Mark walks down the hall.

When Mark opens the door, I can hear the bass from Trevor's car.

Who needs that much bass, like, ever?

I slip past my mom and to the cupboard, where I grab a box of saltines and tuck them under my arm.

"Dinner is at six thirty," she says, "Georgia, you know you don't need a snack."

I shove a saltine in my mouth. "I skipped lunch."

Don't buy saltines if you don't want me to eat them. Just sayin'.

My mom stabs at the chili iceberg some more. She's wearing her yoga pants and her old yoga shirt that has the yoga elephant logo she designed for the studio down the street on the front. This outfit means she's been drawing all day. I don't ask what she's working on because, honestly, I have no interest in hearing what part of my life is being pillaged for the learning experience of children.

"Hey," I say, "did you know some kid at Mark's school was murdered?"

My mom spins around. She puts down the spoon and grabs my shoulders. "I *did* know," she says, in kind of a moany voice. Then she hugs me. She smells like pencil shavings and beans. "God, it's a horrible world. Stay safe, okay?"

"Okay."

When she's finished, my mom releases me and goes back to mashing dinner.

I go to the basement and click on the TV. Mark's laundry is in a pile on one of the cushions. It's mostly socks. I cover it with a blanket because it's weird looking at a pile of socks that still look dirty frankly. Ew.

On TV there's yet another show about murder. An investigator is squatting in a forest next to a tarped gray and blue body, nestled among a thicket of greenery.

The investigator's face twists in anger. "Fucking monsters."

It is hard not to think about a boy being killed

when almost every show on TV is about murder, and I watch a lot of TV.

Someone at school said Todd was found in the snow wearing nothing but a pink mitten, which feels like something you'd see in a movie. The only other thing I heard about Todd is that he didn't have any friends. Which I heard from Taylor Savory, who, like everyone else at St. Mildred's, dates boys from Albright so I guess she would know. Taylor wasn't talking to me, just loudly.

"It's so sad," she said, twisting her long red hair around her index finger. "Apparently, like, NO ONE liked him?"

I'm well aware that this is probably also how someone would describe me if I was found in the woods with nothing but a mitten.

I wonder if the kids at Albright had another name for Todd.

I wonder if a person with no friends can still know their killer?

Sure, right?

Curled up on the couch, suddenly my fingers are chili iceberg cold.

TODD
THE INCIDENT

THREE DAYS INTO THE INVESTIGATION, the following had been determined: Todd did not use social media. He didn't have a blog or a website.

He had a school email account but hadn't used it in almost two years. He didn't have a personal email account. He had the cell phone his mother bought him, but this was still missing. No text messages.

Generally, the only people who ever called him were his mother and his dentist. His mother was the last person to call him, at 1:35 a.m., by which time, the medical examiner determined, Todd was already dead.

"Jesus, are we supposed to be combing his room for telegrams?" Greevy grumbled.

Todd pictured himself like that cartoon of the

humanoid broom and dustpan that walks around sweeping up after itself.

Only one other phone call, the night of the murder, from a burger place at 6:18 p.m., which, the owner explained to police, no one saw because they were slammed that night so anyone could have used the delivery phone to make a call. It was on the far end of the counter. No security cameras. A thousand finger-prints if they bothered to look.

All the local sex offenders—totaling two: one who had previously assaulted a young woman, one who dealt in child porn—were accounted for. Both were out of town with alibis on the night of the murder.

And so, on Saturday, Greevy and Daniels were headed back to the academy, with the radio playing "Manic Monday" by the Bangles.

"What's the teacher's name again," Greevy asked, flipping through her notes.

"Mr. McVeeter."

Todd noted when Mr. McVeeter walked into the staff room to talk to Daniels and Greevy that he looked like shit. Not that McVeeter was a handsome guy. He wasn't. He was shortish, stocky, by his own description, with curly orange hair. "Not exactly

GQ," he used to say. "More like *Better Homes and Gardens*."

But today Todd thought McVeeter looked like actual crap.

Food poisoning, Todd thought. Right.

McVeeter made a strong effort to play the part of someone who wasn't about to puke. When he saw Greevy and Daniels in the staff room, he smiled and picked up his step and held his hand out for hearty handshakes. But he was doing something with his mouth, a twitch, that made Todd pretty sure he was going to puke. Or had puked. Recently.

"Hello there!" McVeeter waved, like Greevy and Daniels had just showed up for a dinner party or something. "Got a meeting in about twenty minutes, hope that's okay. Busy Saturday for a teacher. You know how it is."

"I thought teachers got Saturdays off." Greevy smiled.

"That's students. Teachers use the weekend to catch up." McVeeter gestured at the empty chairs in the lounge. "Please. Wherever you want to sit."

He was green. Like actually green. Like a hospital wall.

Daniels and Greevy sat in the two chairs opposite the couch.

Sitting on the couch, McVeeter offered a weak smile and pointed at the tiny kitchenette. "Can I get you something? They have a, uh, ancient box of Earl Grey and a kettle in here somewhere."

"We're good. Twenty minutes should be plenty. So Todd was a student of yours?" Greevy began, pulling out her notepad.

"Yes." McVeeter wiped his lips with a napkin he'd had wadded up in his palm. Tossed it in the trash. "Todd was, uh, in modern history this year. I teach history and social sciences and I, uh, had the privilege of having Todd in my classes for the past three years. He also worked with me on a tutoring program I set up for students struggling in social science, which I suppose Spot already mentioned."

Greevy nodded. "We understand Todd was a very strong student."

"Yes. He—he was very smart." McVeeter looked at Greevy then at Daniels, like he was watching a tennis match. "He had a great future ahead of him."

"That's why you had him working on this tutoring thing?" Daniels asked.

"Y-yes." McVeeter nodded. "He was my top student. I thought he could help the other students who were struggling a little."

"Was it successful?" Greevy asked.

McVeeter shrugged. "Hard to say. It hasn't run for very long."

Daniels leaned forward. The couch was deep, and Daniels had to almost bend himself in half to get closer to McVeeter. "Do you have any information on what Todd might have been doing on the night of January twentieth?"

McVeeter shook his head. "I don't."

"We're having trouble getting information about Todd, partly because we're having trouble finding students here who knew him or were close to him," Greevy said, holding her hands out in a curious gesture. "So was he more a 'hang out with the teachers and staff,' 'volunteering for school things' kind of kid?"

Todd thought about what McVeeter looked like his first year, when Todd was in grade nine.

Todd sort of hated him that year but couldn't say why. Maybe because McVeeter was loud or silly sounding. Maybe because McVeeter was easily frustrated, an easy target. Most teachers at Albright seemed impervious to student bullshit, or bullies themselves. With McVeeter, when the students acted up, you could see the muscles in his neck twitching when his lips pressed tight, the blood crawling up from his collar to his hairline. You could see him sweat. So kids did things, like drop books, scrape their chairs against the floor, to see McVirgin twist.

Todd hated him until one day McVeeter was the only person at school he could possibly talk to.

"I suppose Todd liked to volunteer. He helped me with a few projects. Model Parliament. The Tutoring League. Aside from that . . ." McVeeter rubbed his face. "I do think he *was* . . . a very private person."

Mr. Doober, the math teacher, opened the door, saw McVeeter, and shut it quickly.

McVeeter held his left hand in his right. You could see a bit of white on his knuckle.

Greevy looked at Daniels. Daniels looked at McVeeter.

"Can I get you a glass of water, Mr. McVeeter?" Daniels offered.

"No, no. I'm fine. I'm sorry. I'm getting over a very bad case of food poisoning," McVeeter said, patting his stomach. "I think it was the chicken."

"Sure." Daniels smiled sympathetically. "I'm wondering, actually, if you can shed some light on something. There was an incident report in Todd's file. I'm wondering if you remember anything about it."

"Spot didn't know?" McVeeter looked surprised.

"He wasn't at Albright during the incident," Greevy said.

"I do . . . know." McVeeter stood up, went to the sink, and got a glass of water. "Todd's student email was hacked. Three years ago. A student, or some students, sent a . . . graphic image to the class. From Todd's email."

"A graphic image?" Greevy asked.

"A picture of a naked . . . A picture of a . . . phallus," McVeeter clarified.

Todd could still picture the giant PENIS. Uncircumcised. A close-up that looked like it was taken with a cell phone. Like it was taken with TODD's cell phone, like he was holding his dick. The subject line was "I like dick."

When he first saw the photo, on his laptop at home, it was like a bomb went off inside Todd's brain.

"Sounds like the sort of thing someone could take pretty seriously, something a school could take pretty seriously," Greevy added.

McVeeter was silent for a second; he pulled his lips tight. "Yes," he said. "You would think so. The school did an 'investigation' but didn't find anyone responsible. I know Todd's mother was very upset but . . . they decided not to pursue it. And Todd . . . Todd was concerned."

"Going after bullies doesn't always work out for the bullied," Daniels said.

Todd's mother *did* want to pursue it. When it first happened, she talked about getting a lawyer. His Aunt Lucy knew a guy and his mother even called him, even insisted Todd talk to him. Then one night they were arguing about it and Todd threw up on the table at dinner, over his untouched potatoes and meat loaf.

After that, she let it go. Which is to say she stopped asking him about it.

"So." Greevy sat forward now, narrowed her eyes at McVeeter. "You could speculate," she continued, slowly, like she was pulling on him. "I mean, I bet you could hazard a pretty good guess at the very least, even if it was just a guess, of who did it."

McVeeter stood and walked across the staff room to his big leather bag with the broken shoulder strap that he sewed together, slung it over his shoulder.

"I don't know," he said. "I'm sorry. I just realized I need to prepare for this meeting. I need to print something."

Greevy and Daniels stood.

"Well, if you can think of anyone in particular"—Greevy handed McVeeter her card—"that you think might know something about what Todd was doing that night, it would help us a lot."

"Of course." McVeeter shoved the card in his back pocket. "Who are you talking to next?"

"We'll be talking to a few members of your tutoring program, since those seem to be the students Todd was closest to."

McVeeter nodded. "If I can be of any help . . . you'll let me know."

Greevy flipped a page over on her notebook. "Can you tell us where you were, incidentally, on the night of Tuesday, January twentieth?"

"I was at home."

Greevy paused, pencil on paper. "Can anyone verify that?"

"Well, I live alone." McVeeter took a deep gulp of air, like a reverse hiccup. "So, no."

"All right then, thank you, Mr. McVeeter." Daniels

nodded. "We'll be in touch if you have any other questions."

"Great. Uh. Okay, good." McVeeter opened the door. "You have my number if you need me."

"We got it." Greevy gave him the thumbs-up.

McVeeter closed the door.

"Pretty bad shakes for food poisoning," Daniels noted.

Greevy hit Daniels with her notebook. "You think incident report dick pic factors into this?"

Daniels looked around the staff room. More pictures of white men, teachers, in gowns of some sort, all with pastoral backdrops. "Dunno. No follow-up on the part of the school, interesting. Seems pretty likely it was another student."

Greevy grabbed a cup and poured a glass of water from the tap. "So we know Todd Mayer, a kid with no friends, was fucked with, clearly, by someone who had a hate on enough to take a dick pic and get into his email. Oh, and we know Todd was a great student."

She slammed her cup down on the counter. "So we have nothing."

"Well"—Daniels tapped his lip—"could be the

reason kid has no email trace. Doesn't use a cell phone. You know, once burned."

"Well, fuck us." Greevy sighed. "We talk to the kids from that tutoring group Monday?"

"Yup." Daniels grabbed his hat from his coat and walked toward the door.

Greevy swiped a cookie from the open box in the kitchen and followed him out and into the hall.

The school was pretty much empty, but for a moment Todd was somewhere in the past, and part of a ghostly memory of a hall full of students, rushing to their next class, streaming through the corridor, surrounded him. For a moment, Todd's ghost was flush with a flashback of indifferent faces in blue blazers, with the odd set of blue eyes catching him sharp like a fishhook as he tried to stay close to the wall, to slide by unnoticed until he could slip into McVeeter's office and disappear.

McVeeter gave Todd the key to his classroom almost two years before Todd died. He gave it carelessly, like it was no big deal, trawled the key ring out of the back pocket of his pants and picked the lint off the ring. It was unusually hot that day, and the furnaces, for reasons no one could explain, blazed, turning the school into an expensive old oven. McVeeter had rolled up his sleeves, was sweating, but was somehow cheerful that day. He threw the key at Todd from his desk while Todd sat at his own smaller desk eating a slightly too-warm-to-enjoy lunch, which his mother insisted on making for him every day because she thought the school stuff was full of sugar.

"Just, use it whenever," McVeeter had told him, from behind his uneven piles of grading and textbooks. "You can come in here, eat. Relax. Plus, you know, I'll need someone to help me with Model Parliament. All good."

He didn't even say why he thought Todd might want a space to eat and feel safe. He didn't ask if Todd was okay. He just threw him a lifeline and smiled, and that was that. Todd hid his relief. He nodded and dropped the key ring into his bag, hearing it hit the bottom with a satisfying metal clunk.

The key to McVeeter's classroom was thinner than most keys, rusted and brassy. The key ring was an Albright Academy keychain like they gave to kids as terrible prizes for reading and being a good sport. It was now in Todd's jacket pocket, somewhere in his closet at home, a closet his mother couldn't look at.

The key had not been entered into evidence, possibly because it was easily mistaken for Todd's house key.

Now, only a few days after his death, the ghost of Todd hovered outside McVeeter's door. Inside, the still-alive-but-feeling-like-death McVeeter was sitting at his desk. Not moving.

The dead cannot apologize.

Just relax, okay?

Outside, it was getting cold.

GEORGIA
COCKTAIL PARTY
REVELATIONS

EVERY FOURTH SATURDAY OF THE month, my mom hosts a party for local children's book illustrators and writers.

Which means every fourth Saturday of the month, my house is flooded with cheese, cut fruit, and wines, all to be consumed by writers and illustrators, in scarves and big necklaces and dresses with loud patterns. My mom never cooks for this event but always wears an apron.

It also means that every fourth Saturday of the month, my dad goes out with his friends to play or watch a sport and, at some point in the day, Mark and I are kicked out of the house or "sent to the store," to buy some weird party thing, like toothpicks or paper straws or butter, which is really about my mom need-ing space before she goes into social mode.

"I can go by myself," I told my mom, when she came downstairs and accosted me on the couch.

"Go with your brother," she shouted, as she strode out of the room in her preparty silk slip and yoga shirt, rejuvenating goop on her face.

Mark stood in the door, resigned. "Come on, G."

The whole way there, Mark keeps his earbuds in and I do, too. His hair is getting shaggy. Pompadour voluminous even. I think he puts gel in it sometimes.

Walking next to my brother reminds me of how ginormous he is, which he suddenly became when he was like twelve and now every year he gets a little more physically intimidating. I think he is mostly protein at this point. Meat and eggs and fruit, which he has pointed out to me is not protein. Although it seems like maybe beets SHOULD be protein.

I wonder if when people see Mark they think he's a bully because he's so big. Of course he's not.

I feel like lately my mom is paranoid that Mark and I don't like each other anymore, because we're not curled up on the couch in our pajamas playing video games on Saturday mornings or conspiring to get my mom to buy sugary cereal at the grocery store.

Because we're not little kids.

The thing is, I don't think Mark and I have to be friends. Like, why is that a requirement? Just because you've written it into a million kids' books, doesn't mean it's true.

Mark is my brother and I have a strong suspicion that if I ever needed his help, he'd grudgingly be there for me—like if I was hanging off a cliff, you know, I think he would pull me up.

Mark is the only person I never have to explain my weird life to. That's enough for me.

I do sometimes think it would be fun to ask him to punch a rock because I saw some guy do it on a YouTube video once and it looked really cool.

It's only when we get into the store and in front of the rows and rows of crackers that Mark pulls out his buds and looks at me. "Wait, what are we getting?"

"Gluten-free crackers," I say, pulling a box of nutty looking things off the shelf and inspecting the label.

"That stuff is all crap," he says, shoving his hands in his pockets. "That gluten-free thing. It's all crap."

Mark hates "crap" food. It's like a personal insult to him. Its existence.

"Well, that's what we're doing." I place the box back on the shelf. "Some people get sick from eating gluten."

"They get sick from eating crap," Mark scoffs.

"Okay, thanks mister in-no-way-helpful guy."

Mark eats BOILED chicken. So he is no help looking for a tasty cracker.

I'm scanning a box of rice crackers when I look up and spot Shirley Mason.

Or I spot Shirley Mason spotting me.

If our parents were with us, we'd have to say hello. If our parents recognized each other or if we were wearing our school uniforms, each of us would get poked in the back, followed by a "Say hello."

I am expecting a stiff, frozen-pizza smile from Shirley. I am expecting a swishy walk, brisk and chilly, noting my existence with a sniff, and then a brush past. Maybe a barely perceptible eye roll because I'm dressed in leggings and a giant sweatshirt. And my puffy coat. Which makes me look like a plum with legs.

Which I KNOW.

I'm expecting this because that is what Shirley Mason does. Has done. For as long as I've known her.

I notice Shirley's hair is not its usually fluffy blond perfection. It's slicked back, which may or may not mean it's dirty, pulled into a feeble looking ponytail. Shirley is holding a bag of oranges, dangling by her side in that thin eco-friendly plastic bag they give you for produce here. Her coat is open and underneath it looks like she's wearing a yellow sweater.

"Just grab whatever," Mark says, looking at his phone.

Down the aisle, Shirley squints at me. Is she squinting or sneering? Whatever it is, it's followed by an abrupt, almost nervous-looking twist and a quick walk in the opposite direction.

All the air has been sucked out of the aisle. I grab a box of the rice crackers, which I'm pretty sure don't have gluten.

"Let's go," I say, walking toward the checkout.

I walk relatively fast, ahead of Mark, pausing in the junk-food aisle, which Shirley would never dare to enter.

Did I mention Shirley Mason once yelled at me in gym that I had monkey legs?

Garbagia and the Monkey Legs. Not a children's book because no one would read that.

You have to LIVE it.

At the checkout counter, Mark's phone starts pinging every six seconds. He walks over to the sliding doors before I finish paying. He's outside, still texting when I walk over, swinging the paper bag with the crackers in it on my finger.

"Uh," he says, not looking up from his phone, "Trevor's gonna meet me here. So, just tell Mom, if she asks, uh, I'm at Trevor's. Okay?"

"Okay," I say, handing him the apple he wanted to buy. "Here."

"Cool," he says, looking at it. "So, uh, is that, you know, that girl by the crackers who was looking at you? Is she, like, a friend?"

I give Mark bug eyes. "My FRIEND?! That was SHIRLEY MASON."

I want him to share my contempt. Not that he will. Why would he? Boys don't care about this shit. Boys care about bananas and the size of their feet or something.

"So what?" Mark takes a giant man-size bite of his apple. "Does she, like, go to your school?"

"Yes, obviously, where else do I meet anyone?" I sigh. "Also. She's a bitch."

"Oh," Mark says, looking at his phone. "Okay. Too bad."

"Are you like offended or something?" I snort. "Are you opposed to sexist slurs?"

"No." Mark rolls his eyes.

"If I hate her, you sort of have to hate her, too, by nature of our blood bond," I say, now testing my hanging-on-a-cliff theory.

Mark rolls his eyes. "Fine. Okay. I hate her. I hate a *stranger*."

I swing my bag some more and watch the shoppers darting out through the thin veil of snow to their cars, bloated bags in tow. "You know," I say, "you're lucky you're a guy and you don't have to deal with girl bull-shit. You couldn't hack it."

"Well, lucky me, I guess." Mark tosses his apple core into the slush with a fastball pitch.

"So," I say, judging this to be the right moment, "this Todd kid. Who was murdered? Was he your friend?"

Mark frowns, fruitlessly digging the toe of his sneaker under a tiny lip of ice. "What do you mean?"

"I mean," I say, "like was he a friend of yours? He was in your grade so—"

"No," Mark cuts in, rubbing his apple-sticky fingers on his coat. He looks down at his phone, which is glowing again. "He wasn't."

"But you knew him?"

Mark frowns. "Georgia. He went to the same school as me, and we're in the same grade. It doesn't mean I knew him. Do you know everyone in your grade?"

"By name or—"

Just then a horn blows, from what feels like inches away. I look over and see Trevor, idling. Staring at us through the window.

"Okay," I say, taking a step backward. "Well, I'll see you."

"Yeah." Mark shoves his phone into his pocket. "Okay. Bye."

On my way home, I get a text from Carrie.

Carrie: If you had to choose between watching a Jane Austen movie or a James Cameron movie which would you watch?

Me: What will you be eating?

Carrie: Fish sticks.

Me: Austen.

Me: Hey so I just saw Shirley Mason at the Safeway and she looked like ☠

Text silence. For four minutes.

Was I being weird? Is she still friends with her? She's not, right?

Carrie: Maybe she's on a diet.

Me: Enjoy your fish sticks.

A couple of hours later, as the party rages on, I am downstairs watching a reality TV show about famous people who are looking for love in all the wrong places and looking through my old school yearbooks, which are normally kept with my mom's books. Solid, leather-bound tomes of child torture shelved next to glittery rainbow books of youthful joy, including her most famous, *You Are Little, I Am Big*.

I have no idea why my yearbooks are down here in the first place, and Mark's yearbooks are in his room.

Maybe mine are still material.

In grade six, the theme of my St. Mildred's yearbook was *Friends Forever*. The picture on the cover is a photo of three girls playing jump rope, a brick wall behind them, the west wall of the middle school.

It is a sunny day on the cover, but all our class photos are grim black-and-white. They look like prison photos of girls in uniform, stacked in rows, glaring at the camera.

I flip through, landing on my class photo. Homeroom 6D.

In every grade from five to ten, I was in the same homeroom as Carrie and Shirley, who, in this photo, sit in the front row, next to each other. Center front. Where you would seemingly put the two most important people. Their knees are pointed toward each other. Their hands rest in their laps. They smile the same knowing smile.

I am in the far-right top corner of this grainy black-

and-white class photo, taken in the school gym, in front of a screen covered with an ivy print. I am looking down. I look like my whole head is hair.

Upstairs, I can hear my mom laughing. I slam the yearbook shut.

Time for a snack!

The kitchen smells like wine and slowly warming dairy. Drunken children's literary figures with jangling bracelets and surprisingly fluffy beards (or both) drift in and out as I peck on bits of cheddar and little baked goods from fancy bakeries still displayed in pink boxes with slightly wilted white paper doilies.

I'm in the process of pushing an éclair into my mouth when I spot the newspaper on the kitchen table, a paper my dad still insists on getting because he thinks the internet is robbing a generation of the ability to read, a paper neither Mark nor I have ever read in the ten years it's been coming to our house. Not that my dad would know this, because he's never around.

The paper is mostly buried in party clutter: a paper plate smeared with what looks like guacamole covers most of the bottom of the front page, a balled-up napkin smeared with lipstick, a few sticky-looking cheese knives, and a half glass of red wine on the corner, but the photo looking out under the headline, "POLICE CONTINUE SEARCH FOR LOCAL BOY'S KILLER," is clearly visible.

The photo is of a boy with black hair, longish in the front. He has dark eyebrows, big eyebrows, like, too big maybe. His face is thin, sharp-edged. He is looking up, from the paper, from my kitchen table, with deep dark eyes.

The boy in it looks nothing like the boy smiling goofy in the photo of Todd Mayer I saw on the news and the internet. This kid is different.

I *know* this kid.

I fucking *saw* this kid.

Here.

He was standing on my front step. A month ago? Before winter break? Maybe just after Halloween. He rang the doorbell, which is maybe why I remember it. Because who rings a fucking doorbell these days? He was wearing this weird long scarf. I remember thinking, *Dude, who just comes by someone's house?*

He had a deep voice. Like adult deep. And he asked for Mark just as Mark reached past me and shoved me into the coats, pulling the boy in by his arm.

I never knew his name.

It's Todd, clearly. Todd Mayer, who is now dead.

What was once a perfectly delicious éclair sticks in my throat like a punch.

Behind me the music switches again to some thumping '80s noise. A sharp voice screams out, "PARTY'S JUST GETTING STARTED!"

TODD
IF YOU CAN BREATHE, YOU CAN LIE

TODD KNEW THAT PEOPLE COULD lie, that many people WERE liars, before he stopped breathing. He knew this before he went to the park where he died, although, not as clearly. He knew this as a ghost hovering over the shrine set up to commemorate his passing, set up by several students, Todd didn't know who, on the front steps of the school, a place that had no significance to Todd.

The shrine consisted of a few candles, white, which bled wax onto the concrete, and a stack of flowers, still in cellophane, carnations you buy at a convenience store. Someone had taped a glossy print out of a picture of Todd, the same one hanging in Greevy and Daniels's office, to a piece of white cardboard and written his name at the top in black marker, all caps. The picture was already streaked from snow.

No one wrote any message. Like, "We will miss you, Todd."

So it wasn't a total sham.

Greevy smoked her third cigarette of the morning standing in front of this memorial, running her finger over the bloom of a carnation from the shrine. A bloom she'd clipped off with the sharp of her thumbnail.

The first official meeting of the Social Sciences Tutoring League, which took place at the end of October and consisted of students who had failed their first two Social Science tests, was a bust.

This fact was not noted in the files of Principal Spot.

It was also not in the files that the league as a group only met twice and that all the students in attendance, including Todd, thought the whole thing was a bad idea.

It's possible that Greevy and Daniels got a sense of the useless nature of the group when they interviewed the members on Monday at lunch period. Greevy certainly seemed to assess that the group consisted of boys that were about as helpful as well-dressed sacks of dirt.

She spent the whole interview with her arms crossed over her chest, looking annoyed.

Chris, Cameron, Mark, and Devon sat in the student lounge and, in no uncertain but almost identical terms, told Daniels and Greevy what everyone had already told Daniels and Greevy: that they didn't know anything about Todd.

It wasn't really a group, they all said. It wasn't like they hung out with Todd.

Devon complained that he hadn't even ASKED for help and he didn't really need it.

Chris said the whole thing was weird.

Daniels asked why. Why was it "weird"?

Chris shrugged, rolled his eyes, and said he didn't want to ask a student for help when they paid good money for trained educational professionals to help them.

A *lot* of good money.

So Daniels and Greevy knew what Todd knew, that Chris was an asshole.

On that first meeting in October, Cameron left halfway through to smoke a joint and never came back. Todd was pretty sure Cameron was also high while he was sitting in his chair talking to Daniels, who sniffed him several times.

Staring at the blank faces of Chris, Cameron, Mark and Devon, Daniels and Greevy couldn't know what it was like to be Todd, standing at the front of the classroom, with a bunch of handouts McVeeter made, screaming on the inside and trying to look on the outside like he, also, didn't give a shit about this whole study group thing.

"Cold as ice" is pretty difficult when you're explaining a handout.

In Todd's mind, the existence of the league illustrated why it was a terrible idea to tell adults anything. Because adults had no solutions, only ideas that made things worse.

Todd had tried to back out of the league when he saw that students had actually signed up, which was when McVeeter informed Todd he'd made the group mandatory for the boys with a failing average.

"They're coming AGAINST their WILL!" Todd screamed.

McVeeter had sat in his office, a fucking traitor without ever knowing it. Like, way to be a safe space while dragging the wolves into the den.

"Todd," McVeeter said, "it's going to be FINE. These kids NEED you. You're going to HELP them. Maybe not all of them but maybe one person will *appreciate* the help and then, you know, you'll have one person who, you know, you can talk to. Bing, bang, boom."

What a ridiculous misunderstanding of human nature, Todd had thought. What kind of a numb brain thinks that kids will be nice to the people who are smarter than them? After the dick pic incident, Todd had spent years being silently brilliant, avoiding any and all formal recognition at Albright. He buried every achievement like a frightened squirrel.

"Give it one week," McVeeter coaxed. "That Mark kid isn't a total dick. He signed up."

Leaving the school after their unfruitful meeting, Daniels and Greevy stood in the teacher parking lot. They'd switched from talking about kids smoking pot at school and whether that was a bad thing per se, to talking about whether to go back to the station or get tacos. Suddenly, Trevor burst out of the front door of the school, with Mark close behind, white shirts gleaming beneath barely buttoned blazers. They jogged a stiff jog to Daniels and Greevy, who turned.

"Look at this," Greevy said under her breath.

Trevor was a good-looking boy. Todd used to think he looked like a thicker, sparklier Brad Pitt. From the first time he saw Trevor, which was his first day of school and also Trevor's, Todd knew Trevor was the kind of person who got what he wanted. Who knew people were going to listen to him, no matter what he was saying. Todd watched Greevy lean back and take Trevor in.

Even the cold seemed to halo around him, like it didn't want to impose.

"Detectives!" Trevor smiled brightly. "I have something. I mean, I think I might have something that could help with the case."

Greevy shoved her lighter back in her pocket, pushing past the carnation, crushed and crispy. "Hi there. And you are?"

"I'm Trevor Bathurst, ma'am. I was a colleague of Todd's, in Todd's homeroom and history class is what I mean." Trevor's wide blue eyes, a helpful look if ever there was a look that could be called helpful. "I wasn't in the tutoring . . . thing, but, I knew Todd. I mean, not close but, you know. I did know him and . . . You said to think about stuff, small stuff? And I thought of something, maybe it would help?"

Mark and Trevor stood side by side, shoulders up, hunched against the chill. Mark shoved his hands into his pockets like he was reaching for heat. Todd watched the space between Mark and Trevor, which seemed carefully maintained.

Trevor smiled an apologetic smile. His teeth chattered slightly. "It's probably nothing."

"But maybe it's not nothing, Trevor," Greevy said, smiling encouragingly, leaning against Daniels's car.

Daniels turned but did not lean against the car, which was covered in winter white salt.

Mark touched his chin to his shoulder. Trevor sighed. "We were just wondering, did you talk to Mr. McVeeter?"

"Your social science teacher." Daniels nodded. "Why do you ask?"

"Just." Trevor took a deep breath. A long breath Todd had seen before, the breath you take when you're about to say something serious to a person of authority, something you want them to take seriously. "Because. I think they were friends. I think Todd and McVeeter were, you know, like *friends*."

"Friends," Daniels repeated.

"*Friends*," Greevy echoed. "How do you know that, if *you* and Todd weren't friends?"

"I suppose . . . I guess I don't completely," Trevor

said, his voice rising at the end. He rubbed his hands together, in an exaggerated fashion, as if to prove he was cold. "I mean, I suppose I saw Todd and him talking, you know, a lot. Outside of class. In the hallways and after. I mean, Todd was super smart so maybe they just had more in common. I don't know. I'm just . . . only because you were asking and I, we, want to help."

Greevy looked at Daniels then back at Trevor. Daniels's face remained still.

Trevor looked at Mark. Mark shrugged.

"Well, that's very helpful, Trevor," Greevy said, her cheeks pink in the cold. "Anything else?"

Trevor gave a long sigh. "Okay, so. Also, I mean, I, WE, saw them having dinner once, outside of school, at this diner. Like, in the fall maybe? Like last fall?"

"Can you remember the name of the restaurant?" Daniels asked, from his perch against the wall.

Trevor paused. He looked at Mark, who was looking at Trevor's shoulder.

"It's not far from the park. I don't know what it's called. On Pine Street. The one with the red and white sign?"

"Great," Greevy said, sliding her notebook in her side pocket. "Well, thanks again. Trevor."

"Thank you," Trevor said, turning back to the school, "you know, for being cops. For keeping us safe."

Greevy watched Trevor and Mark bolt back to the door, blasting past the shrine. Todd wondered if Trevor could feel Greevy's eyes on him, the weight of a finger.

"Got that?" Daniels asked, rubbing his hands together.

"Detectives not cops," Greevy corrected, watching them go.

"You do look like a COP." Daniels grinned, as he pulled open the car door.

"It's the cigarettes," Greevy scoffed.

When Daniels and Greevy got back to the station, the autopsy report was in. They headed to the examiner's office, where they were handed an official-looking piece of paper.

It was a blow to the head, the examiner said, as Daniels read. But the angle suggested a contusion as the result of a fall.

"An accident?" Greevy asked the examiner, a little incredulous.

"Possibly. But that's not what killed him," the examiner said, running his hand through the wiry bush on his skull. "Hypothermia."

"Hypothermia." Daniels looked at the paper.

Greevy shivered.

Todd . . . Just relax, okay?

"He froze to death," Greevy said. "How long after the blow?"

I'm going to get help.

"A few hours."

I promise.

GEORGIA
WHAT MOLLY SAW IN THE WOODS THAT DAY

SO NOT THAT ANYONE'S ASKED me about it since I got home (really all anyone seems to care about is that I bring the laundry downstairs), but today was actually a very interesting day at school.

And by interesting, I mean stressful.

Basically, in gym today, Shirley Mason and Laurie Calberg were the team captains for volleyball, because Laurie and Shirley are always team captains. Shirley because she's popular and Laurie because she's super fucking competitive at even volleyball.

Not me.

First round, Shirley picked Carrie to be on her team. And Laurie, near the very, very end, picked me. Because

I suck at volleyball as everyone should suck at volleyball because it's a horrible sport.

"Have fun," Carrie said, as she ducked under the net to the other side of the court.

"Always," I said, with I think an appropriate amount of dry wit.

I figured Shirley picked Carrie to be on her team to piss off Laurie, because Carrie can actually PLAY. I chalk Carrie's overall ability to play sports to her years as a popular person. I'm pretty sure a huge part of being popular is a knowledge of sports that are professionally played in fashionable Lycra short shorts, but played in green track pants and golf shirts at our school, because that's sort of the punishment of being at this school. Mostly everyone wears their shirts too big or way too small so you can see everyone's nipples in this way I find really distracting.

Everything was volleyball status quo until the point in the middle of the game (which was a tie because Laurie was basically playing every position on our side of the net) when I looked across the gym and I saw Shirley and Carrie talking. Not obviously, like, they were still looking ahead with their arms in the volleyball position, but they were clearly talking to each other. In between serves, Shirley inched closer to Carrie, then away and then closer. Carrie looked dead ahead. But I saw her lips moving.

It looked like how you would talk to someone if you don't necessarily want anyone to know you were talking.

And like, suddenly, the whole day fell into my stomach like a ton of rocks, a feeling I think is a pretty common feeling for teenage girls, the feeling that goes with watching someone you think is your friend do something that means they might not be your friend anymore.

I'm sure Shirley Mason never had this feeling. It smells like wet tinfoil and drool on a pillow.

After gym, I pretty much felt like complete shit, and I kind of stalled in this way I used to do all the time by walking around the gym, pretending to look for something. (I usually tell gym teachers it's an earring.) When I got to the changing room, Carrie and Shirley were gone. Like, they must be the fastest changers ever. I threw on my clothes and left the locker room and walked down the hallway. And because I'm the second-fastest changer ever and fourth period wasn't over, the halls were all quiet. Like all you could hear was the odd squeak of a sneaker, the jangle of a locker door. And then I heard something else; an echo tumbling down the hall, bouncing off the shiny white walls. Shirley's voice.

And Carrie's.

I couldn't tell what they were saying, but it was coming from the stairwell at the end of the hall. It sounded kind of . . . tense. I tiptoed over to the door, and I spotted them through the little webbed glass window. The side of Carrie's face. Shirley's arm.

That's when my shoe squeaked against the floor and they both looked up. The glass was murky, but I could see Shirley's eyes as she spun around and charged toward me.

She slammed open the door with both hands.

"Mind your own business, GEORGIA!" she spat, and charged past me down the hall.

"What was that?" I looked at Carrie, who was standing in the doorway.

Carrie rolled her eyes. "It was nothing. Shirley freaking out. Fuck her."

Then the bell rang and everyone poured into the hallway. Carrie shrugged and headed back to the gym.

Fuck Shirley?

I gotta say it, hearing Carrie say that was basically like the best thing I'd ever heard.

Whatever Shirley's bullshit was, Carrie was MY friend now, hooray.

I practically skipped to my next class.

After school, Carrie came by my locker to tell me she couldn't hang out because she had to go to the dentist.

"I might have dentures tomorrow," she said, tightening her scarf. "So. That might affect our friendship, I don't know."

"We'll figure it out," I said, dragging my coat out of my locker while holding back the ton of crap in there with my foot. "Plus, I heard dentures are cool now."

"I mean, that's what they tell you." Carrie stopped and looked behind me into the chasm that is my limited private space in the school. "Your locker is like . . . a mess."

"I know," I said, slipping into my coat with as much grace as a coat this size allows.

"Later." Carrie grinned, punching my purple sleeve.

"Later GUMS."

I thought that was a pretty good one. Also because . . . gum.

Carrie snorted and trotted off to have her teeth pulled. I headed to the bus stop past Shirley and her crew of girls all huddled around her. She gave me a squinty look, but it pinged off my massive coat like my massive coat was suddenly armor and not embarrassing, and I trotted out the front door.

Screw you, Shirley Mason.

Carrie is cool and I am cool and we are friends.

At home, the first thing I do is get the laundry over with, my weekly chore based on my mom's belief that a grown person should be able to clean up after themselves. Mark and I rotate. It's my turn.

Normally Mark leaves his basket outside his room, but today it's not there so I hammer politely but firmly on the door. "MARK! DUDE! LAUNDRY!"

On my fifth hammer, the door swings open and I realize Mark's not home. He's probably with Trevor.

I don't like Trevor, though, because the first time I ever met him, he sized me up and then looked at Mark with this weirdo wide-eyed innocence and said, "Wow, you guys are like different . . . sizes."

I spot Mark's laundry basket by the bed and step inside.

Downstairs, I can hear my mom with her book agent and best friend, Debra, who is wearing her gold outfit and leaving a smear of lipstick on our wine glasses because she has to dress up like an extra from a Broadway musical every time she comes over.

I hate Debra because she calls me Molly, like *I Am Little and You Are Big*, Molly. I think she thinks it's cute. It was also Debra's idea, back in the day, to dress Mark and me up as our fictional counterparts for my mom's lit tour. I'm not saying that's a bad idea; I'm saying it's clearly an open wound I no longer want poked.

Mark's room is a jock room. There's a set of dumb-bells on the carpet and a bunch of other exercise stuff, including these huge rubber bands that just look like some giant took its hair out of a ponytail and left the band on Mark's floor. There's also the HUGE flat-screen TV Mark used his driveway-shoveling money to buy a few months ago. Which my dad totally lost his shit over (maybe because my dad is jealous because it's a REALLY nice TV).

Grabbing the laundry basket, I notice Mark's schoolbooks are stacked up on his desk with a bunch of papers next to a stack of thick envelopes from different colleges, which started arriving last year. On top of the books is a take-out bag that says Mac's Burgers in bright red neon-style lettering.

I realize I haven't stood in this room in, like, forever. It smells like boy. Like AXE body spray and BO. It feels super fucking weird. It feels like a hotel because of the TV that takes up the whole of the west wall.

What am I doing?

I'm standing in Mark's room; I'm looking for something other than the laundry basket I already have in my hand.

Because this is not a normal laundry day. It's the laundry day after I realized that Todd Mayer had been in this house.

Which is something I have been thinking about all day except for when I was thinking about Carrie and Shirley.

Todd Mayer was absolutely definitely in this house.

Does that make Mark's room a crime scene? No.

If it did, I would be rifling. Right? In cop shows, the cop always walks into a room and starts rifling.

But I'm not going to rifle through Mark's stuff. Because what's Mark done other than lie about a kid he knew?

I hear my mom and Debra laughing downstairs. Caterwauling, my mom calls it.

I do not rifle. But I do turn in place, slowly, walking through my memory of that day like it's the sepia-toned flashback in a movie.

They were at the door. Then I went into the kitchen? I think. And they definitely went upstairs. So Todd was here IN THIS ROOM.

My eyeballs graze over exercise bands, a stack of protein bars, resting on the Mac's Burgers bag, perched on top of *Social Movements in American History*.

The bag is weird for two reasons. One, it's weird because Mark is so super paranoid about what he eats. He ONLY eats like such specific stuff when he's training, and he's always training.

Two, it's not greasy, which is what it would be if you had a big juicy Mac Burger in it or a large or even a small fries. I know this as someone who has left French fry boats in her pockets and in other places and so has many things that smell like grease in her closet and on her floor.

And it's not crinkly, like how a bag would be if you put fries in it then grabbed it by the top. Instead it looks like it's been folded in half and folded again. Like . . .

I step over to the desk, unfold the top of the bag, look inside and see . . . money. Lots of money.

"What's all this money doing here?" asked little sister Molly.

"It's just money," big brother Wally said. "Lots of people have money. What are you doing in my room?"

The thing about Molly is, she literally doesn't know anything, the whole walk through the woods. Then when they get to the old lady's house at the end of the story, Molly thinks the old lady is a witch. Big brother Wally knows there's nothing to be afraid of. Big brother Wally says there's no witches, just old ladies with gardens who bake cookies.

But Molly won't eat the cookies because that's a big no-no, writing stories where kids eat stranger's baked goods. While big brother Wally tells the not-witch about all the things they saw in the forest, Molly just sits there.

So maybe Molly's not totally out to lunch.

"GEORGIA!"

TODD
A TALE OF TWO TODDS

TODD KNEW, WHEN HE WAS alive, that a person is never just one person. There's the person you are in front of people, and the person you are when you are alone.

As a ghost, Todd spent a lot of time in rooms with people who thought they were alone. He watched Greevy sit in bed watching movies on her laptop and smoking, stabbing endless cigarettes out on a big brown ashtray that looked like a school craft project. Greevy, alone, bought multiple microwave dinners and then ate only the bits she liked out of each of them, like a food puzzle. A very wasteful food puzzle.

She watched romantic comedies starring Sandra Bullock and chatted with men on dating apps on her phone, leaving what Todd thought were vague but leading messages for multiple possible dates.

Todd sometimes wondered if she could see him, hovering in the blue glow of her laptop, which was sometimes the only light in the room other than the amber ember of her cigarette.

Daniels was rarely alone. He had a chubby, blue-haired boyfriend who wore superhero T-shirts Todd found shocking because Daniels only wore really nice things. The boyfriend was always playing upbeat dance music. The kind of music that goes with some-one blowing a whistle in time to the beat. The chubby boyfriend liked to dance in the living room in his bare feet. Sometimes Daniels danced with him, muted but happy.

While he was alive, and now, Todd knew that McVeeter was not the same person he was at home that he was at school.

When McVeeter took Todd out for a thank-you dinner for helping out with Model Parliament, they chatted about everything but school. He asked Todd about the kind of movies he liked. He told Todd about a good podcast about old Hollywood. Todd suspected McVeeter was worried about him. McVeeter told Todd he'd known Todd had been through a lot, meaning the dick-pic thing and, Todd suspected, everything else that had to do with what McVeeter thought it meant for Todd to be gay at Albright.

He looked so serious, at the end of dinner. When he gave the waitress his card, he turned to Todd and told him if he ever needed *anything* he just had to ask.

"I *don't* need anything," Todd told him.

"Well," McVeeter said, pocketing the receipt. "When you do, you'll tell me."

That was also the first time Todd ever saw McVeeter's apartment, if only from the doorway while he waited for McVeeter to retrieve a book from his living room, on Danish cinema. At the time it just seemed like one of those weird moments, like a break in reality where suddenly teachers have homes and lives.

He didn't think about McVeeter a lot, if he was honest, even if he was one of only two people Todd actually talked to at school. He was just the guy that seemed to want Todd to be happier. Of course, this was before Todd realized how much McVeeter wanted Todd's life to be better. And what that would mean for the both of them.

Now, at the police station, in a place that seemed far away from everything else, McVeeter looked uneasy.

"Thank you for coming in," Daniels said, pointing to the chair at the far side of the table in the interview room.

"Of course." McVeeter wore his blue sweater and work cords. He sat with his hands clasped on the top of the table.

Greevy smiled and put a paper cup of water in front of McVeeter, before settling into her chair.

"Just a few questions," she said.

Daniels leaned against the wall by the door, next to the mirror that wasn't really a mirror.

"Whatever I can do to help," McVeeter said, brushing his fingers over his top lip, wiping away a thin layer of sweat.

"When we spoke a few days ago," Greevy said, looking at her notebook, "you told us that you taught Todd. We now have a witness who says he saw you with Todd outside of class. Did you spend time with Todd, outside of school?"

"I have . . . I did." McVeeter crossed his arms over his chest. "That's very . . . broad. Do you want to be specific?"

"We have a witness who says he saw you and Todd at a restaurant last year," Greevy said.

"Are you implying that there's something wrong with that?" McVeeter pressed his fingers into his biceps.

Daniels cleared his throat.

"Did you take Todd out to dinner?" Greevy asked, tilting her head. "Often?"

"I don't like the wording you're using here detective. I might have . . ." McVeeter leaned forward, rested his forearms on the desk, "purchased dinner for Todd after a night of working on a school project. It was . . . September. I think September fifteenth. We'd just finished Model Parliament. He was a volunteer. That's . . . That's it. There's nothing wrong with that. I can get a receipt for you if you need it."

"You don't buy dinner for every student, do you?" Greevy added, pushing a hair behind her ear. "I'm assuming."

"Not on a teacher's salary, no," McVeeter said, sitting back in his chair. "Next question?"

"A teacher at your school," Greevy said, moving on swiftly, "said they heard you in a confrontation with

Todd a week before his murder. Can you tell us about that?"

Todd looked at McVeeter. His neck was turning purple. "Who said that?"

"What were you upset about?" Greevy asked, blinking away McVeeter's question. "That day? Do you remember?"

"I wasn't upset," McVeeter said evenly. "I never had a confrontation to Todd. This is a fiction."

Mrs. Cuspin, the music teacher, had taught at Albright for twenty years. She wore pencil skirts that hugged her generous butt, soft silk blouses with floral prints that hugged her generous . . . chest, and her hair in what was essentially a beehive, something that seemed to endear her only to Todd, who could not sing but loved watching Mrs. Cuspin's head bob in time to the music. She also wore glasses on a pearl chain that hung around her neck, rarely on her face. McVeeter said she was vain.

Mrs. Cuspin liked to wander the halls at lunchtime, with a pink mug of the staff room's ancient, and, as McVeeter often noted, tasteless tea. Todd had seen her peering into McVeeter's office, her nose an inch from the class, to see who was doing what. McVeeter used to wave at her, an exaggerated, cheerful wave, like you'd give standing on a ship leaving port.

"HELLO, MRS. CUSPIN! HOW'S YOUR HOT BROWN WATER?"

She never waved back.

"Nosy old cow," McVeeter would snort, watching her clip away.

McVeeter said Cuspin had a grudge against old queens. Which was unfair, McVeeter said, since she was also clearly an old queen.

"Did you and Todd ever fight?" Daniels asked, not budging from his spot on the wall. "Have an argument?"

The words Mrs. Cuspin told the detectives she heard McVeeter yell were, "You are a cheat and a liar. A CHEAT and a LIAR."

She repeated it with the exact cadence and emphasis ("Exact," she said) to the detectives that morning, pointing to the spot in the hallway, right next to the elbow of hall that turned from the North Wing of the school to the West Wing. She told the detectives she had always thought McVeeter had a loose interpretation of professionalism, but she was shocked to know it went beyond that.

"What does that mean?" Greevy asked Mrs. Cuspin, leaning forward to see what Mrs. Cuspin must have seen that day. "Went beyond that?"

"It means that we are *teachers*, Detective Greevy. Educators. Icons. When I came to Albright, it was a code of conduct. But teachers nowadays would like to see themselves as friends of students. Which is an immature notion,"—Mrs. Cuspin shook her head—"with grave consequences."

"What would we have to fight about?" McVeeter's voice simmered under the fluorescent lights of the interview room. "What would I POSSIBLY have to fight about with Todd Mayer?"

Greevy shifted in her seat, looked at McVeeter with a constant, steel gaze. "Maybe you had a relationship with him that was beyond what a student normally has with their teacher? Maybe this relationship went further than you meant it to? And you fought—"

McVeeter stabbed his finger on the desk, his voice boiling over now. "This is disgusting, what you are doing right now. This is homophobic, at the least, to suggest, that because Todd was a gay student and I am a gay man, to SUGGEST that that somehow means that I would have any feelings, any RELATIONSHIP with a SEVENTEEN-YEAR-OLD BOY is VILE."

"Mr. McVeeter," Daniels said quietly, "we are asking these questions because we are trying to find out—"

"I was his TEACHER," McVeeter boomed. "I was there for him AS A TEACHER. I was—"

"We have a witness," Greevy cut in, looking sympathetic, "who is suggesting that you had a conflict with Todd. That a week before his death you confronted him in the hallways of school. If you can clear up for us what that would have been, then we can get to the bottom of what happened to him that night. We have leads that open up, Mr. McVeeter, that we need to pursue. This is nothing more than that."

"This incident never happened," McVeeter said, "so whoever told you that is LYING."

For a good minute, everyone sat in silence. Including Todd, who had everything to say and nothing to say, because he was dead.

"This is discrimination." McVeeter said, finally, sitting back in his chair. "Unless you have any more ridiculous questions, I'd like to leave."

Greevy stood, and she and Daniels left the room.

McVeeter put his palms down on the table and looked at his hands in silence for a long time. A small shadow of heat radiated out of his palms. He closed his eyes.

"Todd," he said, to the empty room, to the ghost of Todd, who felt every word, a unique sensation in his current state. A Q-tip on his soul.

"Todd . . ."

It's okay.

When Todd was in grade ten, McVeeter started throwing pens. He'd throw it on the ground, so hard sometimes the caps shattered. It was how he got kids to stop dropping things when he was teaching. The first time he did it, he told Todd, it freaked students out.

"I know what it means to put on a front," he said. "I bark like a mad dog in class so students think I'm crazy and they don't give me shit. So I GET it, Todd."

It seemed important to McVeeter that Todd got that McVeeter got Todd. Which at first didn't seem to Todd to be a helpful thing. So McVeeter got Todd? So what?

Mark had told Todd that most of the students were scared of McVeeter.

"But you're not, right?" Mark asked. "I mean . . . because you guys are like, friends or whatever. Right?"

At the time, Todd flushed red. Friends? Mark thought Todd and McVeeter were friends? What else did Mark think?

Todd could guess.

"We're not friends," Todd said. Todd didn't know what else to say to make it clear that whatever Mark was thinking wasn't what was happening. So he just rolled his eyes.

The last time he saw McVeeter, the last time he was in McVeeter's apartment, where no one could see them and certainly Mrs. Cuspin was nowhere around, McVeeter sat in his chair, in his slippers, and his sad blue school sweater, worn cords, and he looked up at Todd, who was standing in the doorway again, because he was afraid to step inside.

Not afraid of McVeeter just . . . afraid. Or maybe it wasn't fear, just, a horrible feeling like fear.

McVeeter didn't yell, he just asked Todd, his voice calm in a way that freaked Todd out even more, "Please just tell me what's happened. I won't be mad, but Todd, I need to know."

Todd remembered staring at his mittens.

"Please, I promise I won't be upset," McVeeter said. "I just don't understand."

Maybe McVeeter was scared that there were two Todds.

Maybe there were.

Maybe that's true of everyone you let into your life, which is why people are dangerous, with their barks and their bites.

Greevy and Daniels returned to the interrogation room and told McVeeter that he was free to go.

Outside the hallway, after the heavy metal door clicked behind them, Daniels put his hands in his pockets. "I don't know."

Greevy pinched the pack of smokes in her pocket. "He looks jumpy to me."

She touched a finger to her lips. "He called Todd a cheat. Maybe Todd was cheating on him . . . like in a relationship?"

Daniels frowned. "In a school setting, could be grades."

Greevy nodded. "Time to call Spot."

GEORGIA
MONEY IN A BAG

IN MY LOCKER, RIGHT NOW, are the following things.

- 1 set of gym clothes. Not washed.
- 1 set of running shoes. Smelly.
- 2 bags of mostly eaten popcorn
- 1 lunch packed by my mom with leftover pizza and a weird hunk of candied fruit in a beeswax wrap
- 1 bag of money

I skipped gym, and now I'm sitting in what I think of as my secret hiding place, which is really just the old booth for the school auditorium that they don't use now because everything is wireless.

I am thinking.

Yesterday when my mom spotted me in Mark's room, I grabbed the bag and a bunch of laundry on the floor and booked it out of there, just about tipping my mom's wine into her shirt.

"What are you doing," she gasped.

"Laundry!" I shouted behind me, as I barreled down the stairs with a basket of lights and darks and Mark's money.

Then I stood in the laundry room and tried to think, but it was impossible with my mom and Debra upstairs caterwauling hardcore and then my dad came home and I just panicked and shoved the bag of money in my school bag and now it's at school.

Mark stayed at Trevor's house last night, so technically I could just put it back in his room after school and it would be no big deal.

So here's a question. Why did I take this fucking bag of money?

Did I take it because a) I watch too many cop shows, b) Mark lied about knowing Todd, or c) I myself am a thief.

Okay, I'm not keeping the money so it's not C.

I did count it. It's one thousand, seven hundred

dollars. Cash. And not crisp, either. Like twenties and stuff.

Could Mark just have that much money on him? I know he does this driveway shoveling thing, but I also know he, like, spent a ton of money on the TV.

Trevor is rich, maybe he got the money from Trevor. But then . . .

Why would he *need* this much cash?

For some reason, it feels like this is the kind of money you give someone to either pay someone off or pay someone to do something for you. Like, a job.

Or drugs?

Or maybe he's buying a motorcycle, Georgia. Geez.

Okay, but the bag is weird. Like, since when does Mark go to burger places? He won't even eat butter on toast because it's outside of his meal plan.

There's no reason to think this money has anything to do with Todd, Georgia. It's just money.

So it's Tuesday, really the worst day of the week anyway, and I am like a cat in a mall all day. Just. Jumpy. What's the best metaphor for that? I don't know.

"Hey," Carrie says, stepping up to me after French, "what is going on with you today? Are you on drugs?"

I grab my bag off my desk. "I'm high on life," I say, instantly regretting it because what does that even mean. "I mean, nothing. I'm . . . just thinking."

"About what?" Carrie asks, following me out of class. "Puppies? The economy? My dentist appointment, which went very well thanks for asking."

Carrie bares her teeth at me.

"Money," I say. "And good to hear."

The halls are sweaty and crowded. Or I'm sweaty and suddenly claustrophobic. Carrie stares at my face.

"You're thinking about money," she says, rounding the corner behind me. "Like savings bonds and stuff? Putting away for a rainy day?"

"Something like that," I say. "Should we get lunch? Let's go out for lunch."

"Okay." Carrie catches up to me. "But you're buying. With your money."

I don't get my coat, because it's deceptively sunny outside and because I don't want to open my locker in front of Carrie. Because money. So we jet outside with me in nothing but my uniform and a prayer. Which I instantly regret, because turns out it's sunny, but it's fucking cold outside. Maybe too cold for the food truck, which is a no-show. Which makes me think of the last time I saw the Fry Guy and wondered whether he killed Todd Mayer.

Back when it was all, "Ha ha, some guy died. I wonder who did it?"

My arms are turning to ice. Like actual blocks of ice as I stand on the sidewalk in front of the school with no coat and no French fries and the blazing winter sky overhead and Carrie standing in front of me waving her arms in my face.

"Earth to Georgia," she says. "Do you want to get your coat? Is your brain frozen? Should I call an ambulance or a therapist or something?"

My fingers are curling up like dead leaves. I shove them in my armpits, which I'm sure looks weird. "Uh . . ."

Carrie scans the horizon of nothing but buildings that don't contain fries. "Or we can sprint six blocks to the hot dog place."

I stamp my feet to life. "Not really a sprinter."

"Are you okay? You seem weirder than normal." Carrie unwraps a piece of gum. I turn and look to see her popping what might be her second or third piece in her mouth.

She looks at me with hard brown eyes, chewing methodically.

"Yeah, it's just . . ."

I'm about to say something, God knows what, when I catch it out of the corner of my eye. What looks like Trevor's SUV, gliding through the gates of the school parking lot.

It is.

"What?" Carrie frowns.

"I know that guy," I say.

The next thing I know, I'm following Trevor's SUV, walking at a solid clip, around the school.

I don't realize I've started running until I feel the little icicle shards in my lungs ringing like baby wind chimes.

Carrie huffs after me. "Georgia! What the fuck!"

The student parking lot curves down next to the west side of the school. It's a pockmarked drive that rocks the SUV like a toy so it slows down enough for me to catch up, before Trevor pulls up past the doors of the back entrance and stops.

It's the part of the school where they do deliveries. Next to the kitchen, off the cafeteria. It's narrow enough that it's going to be hard to back out of without scraping his precious car on the abundance of brick and concrete.

I am standing next to a wall, around the bend from where he's stopped. Just out of sight. I assume. Although maybe if I can see him, he can see me. But I don't think he's looking. His car is idling, huffing its standard emissions of a lake's worth of pollution. He's probably looking at his phone. Carrie steps up behind me, breathing heavily. I can smell orange and grape and hear a smack of a small bubble just as Shirley steps out of the cafeteria doors and walks up to Trevor's car. The car window opens. She doesn't lean on the door. She's wearing a leather jacket with a fur-lined hood. She's wearing knee socks. Her hair looks perfect. She stands back, looking inside.

Carrie smacks another bubble.

After a minute, the passenger side door opens, and Mark gets out of the car and gets into the back seat while Shirley gets into the front.

"Huh," I say. "That's Mark."

Carrie looks at me. "*That's* your brother?"

I turn and look at Carrie. "What?"

Carrie shrugs. "Nothing. I've never met him before so just—"

"Does Shirley Mason know Mark?" I ask.

Carrie frowns. "Does Mark know Trevor Bathurst?"

I nod.

"Yeah. Well. Shirley goes out with him. Or went out with him. Maybe she still does." Carrie stomps her feet. "Can we get food now?"

I'm following Carrie back to the sidewalk, trying to think. What did Mark say at the grocery store? I'll tell you what he didn't say. He DIDN'T say, "Hey, that girl you're talking about is dating my best friend."

He said something about a stranger. Like, about why would he hate a stranger?

"So you know Trevor," Carrie says.

"Yeah, he's friends with Mark." I frown.

"Then Mark is an idiot," Carrie says, "because Trevor Bathurst is a dick."

TODD
TWO, THREE, NINETEEN

THERE ARE THINGS THAT ARE a secret that everyone knows. Like that the wrestling coach, Mr. Winter,
was fucking the Religious Ed teacher, Mrs. Habler, even
though they were both married. Todd found out because
one day the door to Mrs. Habler's office was locked and
he made the mistake of looking in the little foggy
window, long enough to catch a note of . . .

Something even his ghost couldn't unhear.

There are secrets at least nineteen people know.

Spot met Greevy and Daniels in the corridor of the
school the next day, looking sweatier than ever, if that
was possible. The first bell had just rung, and students
swirled through the hallways.

Spot pushed past them, focused on Greevy and Daniels.

"Detectives, please, follow me."

This time, he did not smile or shake their hands, but pivoted and charged in quick, small steps down the hall.

In Spot's office, Greevy unconsciously wiped her top lip, watching the sweat trickle-down Spot's face as he settled behind his desk. It looked like he'd been sitting in a sauna for an hour. He pulled out another of his file folders, this one crisp. New. He took a deep breath. Placed the folder on the desk.

"Of course, you understand that we do not, we would not have . . ." Spot shook his head. "This is an unpleasant surprise to say the very least. This kind of behavior is in no way condoned by Albright Academy."

Outside the window, a herd of students huffed past in a serious jog, their cheeks red with cold. Mr. Winter working the grade elevens with what he called "cold therapy." Todd watched the puffs of air stream from their noses and lips.

Greevy, standing to the left of the desk, put her hand on the folder. "May I?"

"Y-yes." Spot pulled his finger off the folder, looking at Daniels as Greevy opened the folder. "After your call, we examined Todd's grades over the past three semesters, and we did not see any anomalies, of course, as I said Todd was a very able student. However . . ."

Greevy's eyebrows went up as she scanned the contents of the file, passing pages to Daniels as she read.

"We did"—Spot paused to clear his throat, an incredibly uncomfortable sound, like a record skipping very slowly—"take a deeper look at the rest of the class grades and discovered . . . an anomaly in relation to Mr. McVeeter's grade-twelve social studies class, which Todd was a member of . . ."

"Nineteen kids went from a C or a D to an A on the last midterm," Daniels said, tapping a spreadsheet.

"Yes." Spot cleared his throat again. "It appears that at least nineteen of our students had a significant jump in their grades for this last exam. We believe this jump was . . ." Spot paused. "Artificial."

"This midterm was when?" Daniels asked, reading over Greevy's arm as she flipped through the pages.

"December fifteenth. It was the last exam of the first term."

"So," Greevy said, "they cheated."

"On this particular exam, it does appear," Spot said, stiffening, "that some sort of nefarious activity took place, for nineteen of the students in the class."

"Pretty much the whole class," Greevy added.

Daniels nodded. "Do you have the exams themselves?"

Spot handed over a larger folder filled with exam booklets. McVeeter hated multiple choice. He told Todd it was the hopscotch of academia, so his exams were always essays.

Todd always found the booklets somewhat satisfying. He used to enjoy running his fingers over the textured covers. He'd always agreed with McVeeter, although they never discussed exams in any detail, that multiple choice was kind of cheating because you could guess and get it right without actually knowing the answer.

You should have to know something to get it right, Todd thought.

Daniels scanned the papers while Greevy tapped her chin.

"Did McVeeter discuss this with you?" she asked, pulling out her notebook. "Flag it? The grades?"

"No, he did not." Spot drummed his fingers on the

desk near the picture of his dog, who smiled back at him from the silver frame on Spot's desk with black lips and sharp white teeth.

"Does he know you're looking at these grades now?" Greevy asked.

"No, he does *not*," Spot said crisply, finally wiping his hand across the slick surface of his brow. "We received your call, and we did a search of the grades for Todd's year and this is what we found. And of course we notified you immediately. We thought . . . I thought it would be prudent to discuss this matter with you first."

"We appreciate your prudency," Greevy said. "Is Mr. McVeeter in school today?"

"He is in class, yes." Spot nodded, pulling up a grid on his computer. "It's Wednesday so he will be in room 454. Until morning break."

"Can you excuse us, Principal Spot?" Daniels tapped the file, looked at Spot. "We just need a moment."

Principal Spot scooted out of his chair with a little more haste than seemed normal. "Of course, I was just about to check in with my assistant. Move some meetings. You may use my office."

When he closed the door behind him, Greevy sprung

up and over to Spot's desk, sinking into his chair. "It's like twenty degrees warmer in this chair," she gasped, plopping her notebook on his desk. "Okay. So. News flash. Rich kids cheat."

"Yup." Daniels flipped through the booklets, running his finger over the answers, often pressed into the page in pencil with such force they left a brail behind. "Hey, look, it's your favorites."

Daniels pulled booklets out of the pile, slapping them on Spot's desk. "Cameron Hill, Chris Mattieu, Devon Marcus . . ."

"All members of an apparently very useless study group," Greevy noted, leaning back in Spot's chair.

"Yep." Daniels nodded; he tossed another booklet on the desk. "And . . . Mark Walker."

Mark Walker had terrible handwriting. Each letter crawled, gasping for breath, across the page to the end of every raggedly disjointed sentence. Todd thought that was why Mark didn't like to take notes, which was part of why he was failing social studies. When Mark sat next to Todd in class, Todd would watch him out of the corner of his eye, his little forelock dangling over his face as he just held onto his pen, staring at the paper like it was talking to him.

Mark was the only person Todd had ever met with hands bigger than his. Mark said it was good for wrestling, for getting a good hold.

"Oh, I think of it as having piano hands," Todd said. "Like for reaching the keys."

"Reaching keys?" Mark seemed stumped. "Don't you just move your hands?"

Todd laughed so hard he almost fell out of his chair. Mark looked embarrassed.

"You know what I mean." Mark rolled his eyes.

This exchange was at an unofficial meeting of the tutor club, that was by then no longer a club and just Mark and Todd. In Mrs. Habler's classroom, which was usually empty at lunch. Mark always sat under the picture of the Sistine Chapel, of God reaching to Man. Maybe that's too symbolic, but that's where they started hanging out. Or, whatever you want to call it.

Todd used to wonder if anyone knew where Mark was when he went to those tutoring sessions. If it was a secret. Mark said he just needed to get his grades up a letter. Otherwise there was no way he could get into college.

That old chestnut.

Daniels thumbed through each exam a question at a time. It didn't take him long to notice the little dots McVeeter used for marking, following along each sentence.

"Look at this," he pointed.

McVeeter had underlined, on Mark's paper, the same sentence he'd underlined on eighteen other papers because they all used it in one form or another.

A person's identity as a citizen, who is part of a community or a country, is a matter of ideology, it tells him what to do and what his responsibilities are.

Except for the gender bit, it was almost verbatim from the reference sheet. Apparently, Mark was pretty good at memorizing.

Apparently, they *all* were.

"Okay, I'm going to say it," Greevy said, looking at the array of exams. "These kids are thick and unimaginative."

Daniels pointed at the red underlines. "McVeeter marked up these papers, underlined this stuff, which means he *knew*," he said. "So why not go to Spot? It's not like it was his fault."

Greevy plopped back into Spot's chair and tilted back until she was staring at the ceiling. "Right? So instead, after the break, he goes after Todd? Calls him a 'cheat and a liar.'"

Daniels frowned. "You think Todd was cheating, too?"

Daniels rummaged in the file and pulled out Todd's exam. Opened it to the same question.

In his exam, Todd wrote:

OUR IDENTITIES AS AMERICAN CITIZENS, AS WELL
AS THE MANY OTHER CULTURES, COMMUNITIES,
AND MICROGROUPS WE CONSIDER OURSELVES TO BE
MEMBERS OF, ARE AS MUCH A MATTER OF IDEOLOGY
AS THEY ARE LIVED EXPERIENCES. WE ARE CITIZENS
BY BIRTH, BUT WE GROW INTO THE PERSON WE
KNOW WE ARE MEANT TO BE, FOLLOWING RULES, OUR
ACTIONS MARKED BY INVISIBLE BOUNDARIES, THE
WEIGHT OF RESPONSIBILITIES.

"Either he cheated WAY BETTER," Daniels noted, "which given his track record would also suggest he cheated all the time, or, more likely—"

"Or he didn't cheat. But we don't know." Greevy shook her head, reading through the rest of the essay.

"But we don't know." Daniels nodded.

It did not bother Todd to think that Greevy and Daniels would think he needed to cheat on a midterm. Because he was dead. Living, it would have made him livid. It was one thing not to want everyone to think you were smart; it was another to have someone think you were so un-smart you had to cheat on a test.

Greevy considered. "Worth talking to the tutor crew again?"

"Let's get the whole class in, everyone who cheated." Daniels stepped toward the door and stopped. "Call their parents, too."

There are things that are a secret that everyone knows.

When Greevy and Daniels entered Todd's former classroom with Spot this time, it wasn't a surprise; their arrival had already hummed through the halls. Before the doorknob twisted, with the shadow of Spot in the doorway, nineteen boys looked at one another across their desks.

As soon as Principal Spot stepped into 234, Mr. Farley's grade-twelve calculus, Chris pulled out his phone and held it up for the detectives to see.

"My father is a *lawyer*," he announced. "I have the right to retain counsel."

"Shut the fuck up, Chris," Devon grumbled from the other side of the classroom.

All the students on the list went to Spot's office to call their parents, then they were seated in an empty classroom, which happened to be Mrs. Habler's.

Mark called his mother, who was working at home. Then he was silent as Daniels pointed him to the chair under a glossy image of the Sistine Chapel. He put his index finger to his lip and bit off a piece of cuticle, which Todd had never seen him do.

Trevor leaned back in the chairs set up for them, looked at the ceiling.

Daniels stood at the front of the classroom, snug in the silence.

"What are we doing?" Cameron finally mumbled, amid a chorus of chair squeaks. "I mean, or whatever."

Todd could see that Cameron was high and pretending not to be high, which seemed to be making it worse.

"We're waiting for your parents," Daniels said, scanning the boys. "And we're all having a think while we sit here. About what we're going to say when your parents get here. Because when they do, *we* are going to have *another* discussion about any relevant details you might have not shared previously that you're going to seriously consider sharing *now* about your fellow student, Todd Mayer, who I will remind you all again, is dead. This cheating thing you all clearly were a part of may or may not have anything to do with Todd being dead, but it seems to me a pretty solid coincidence, which I don't believe in."

Mark looked at his hands.

It's possible Daniels, as a detective, knew what Todd had only learned just before his untimely demise, that a secret is rarely a secret for long.

Because people are careless.

Trevor sat up in his chair and stretched. He looked over at Mark on the other side of the classroom. Mark looked at Trevor then looked away.

People being careless is how two students becomes three students, and how three becomes five becomes nineteen.

This particular secret, split three ways, wasn't a ton of money but it was something, is what they told Todd.

And Todd was careless, too, so he agreed.

GEORGIA
WEDNESDAY AND OTHER
FUCKED-UP THINGS

IT'S WEIRD HOW LISTENING TO people yell at people is fascinating, because people actually yelling at *you* is terrifying. When you're not the target, it's intense but totally watchable.

One moment everything was fine. Girls in the cafeteria, eating soup, or, because it's Wednesday, lasagna, which is okay but not great. People in their little groups, Shirley and her crew, and me and Carrie in the corner.

Then the next minute, Shirley was screaming at Sarah Hammersmith about what, I wasn't clear. But unless what Sarah said was "Your hair's on fire," it was a clear overreaction.

Carrie looked up from her meatballs. "What the fuck?"

Shirley, tears streaming down her face, stomped her foot. "Fuck you, Sarah." She wiped her eyes, a little bit of mascara running. "FUCK YOU, you WHORE."

"Did Shirley just call someone a whore?" I gasped, actually legitimately surprised because . . . like wow, really? A whore? What was this, church?

Sarah gasped, hand on chest. "Fuck, Shirley. I was just ASKING."

"Nobody cares about ME," Shirley spat, storming out of the room.

Carrie munched her pie. Then looked at me. "You want ice cream?"

"It's like minus thirty degrees."

"That's a no, then?"

I might not be screaming my head off in the cafeteria but I also have a problem, in the shape and form of the bag of money that is still stuffed in my locker. Money I didn't take home and did not give back to Mark last night.

I could have.

I did not.

This is, to be clear, a problem, in part because I'm pretty sure Mark now knows that his money is missing but he hasn't said anything about it. He didn't even ask if the woman who cleans the house moved it, which is what I would do if I had a legitimate pile of money and it suddenly went missing.

He did look at me, for like twenty seconds when he came downstairs for breakfast this morning with his big floppy gym bag that he dropped on the floor in front of the kitchen table.

At first, I thought he was looking at me like in some sort of accusatory way because I'm basically in some sort of tell-tale heart situation right now. But then I looked up from my cereal and realized he was like practically asleep; his eyes were almost closed and he was all greasy.

"Mark," my dad tutted, smoothing down his tie as he stood up from the table, "you need to shower."

"Yeah, I have practice at school then I'll shower," Mark said.

"Hey, Mark," I said, salutary.

"Hey, G," he sighed, grabbing a banana from the table.

Then he slipped out the front door to grab a

ride with Trevor. Who was blasting "Welcome to the Jungle" so loud in his car I could hear it in the kitchen.

After Shirley's meltdown, we had independent study. Carrie and I worked on our bio presentation in the Hall C alcove. Which seemed like a good chance to ask Carrie about something I have been thinking about that I cannot google for any sort of helpful answer.

"Hey," I said, leaning over my desk.

"Hey, what?" Carrie whispered, her nose an inch from her book.

"Why do you think a person puts money in a paper bag?"

Carrie looked up. "Is this like a riddle? Like why did the chicken put his money in a paper bag?"

"Or her. Why is the chicken a 'he'?"

"Sure, or her. Chicken her. A hen with a lot of money," Carrie muses.

"It's a hypothetical question," I cut in. "But we can make it a riddle if you want."

"I guess, to give to someone," Carrie said, as she slipped a tab of gum between her lips and began surreptitiously chewing. "But in a weird way. My stepmom uses weird things as envelopes like brown paper bags and shit like that. But she's crafty."

"Right," I said, lowering my voice. "Does your step-mom give people money in recycled envelopes made of, like, cut up cereal boxes?"

"She usually writes a check," Carrie said, now searching my face. "Wait. Are you giving me money?"

"You're rich, and you want me to give you money?" I asked.

"You brought it up." Carrie shrugged. "And I'm not rich. My dad is rich."

"Which is something pretty much every girl in this school has said at one point."

"HA!" Carrie laughed so hard she spit out her gum. "Too fucking real, Georgia."

After school, Carrie wanted chicken nuggets so we walked the eight blocks to McDonald's. Is it me or is most of socializing getting food?

Once she was full of batter and chicken, on our way back to the bus stop, Carrie looked at me out of the side of her eye and asked, "Why do you want to know about bags of money? Are you selling drugs? That's also a money bag thing."

"I'll tell you," I said, finishing my milkshake, fingers numb in the cold, "if you tell me why you're not friends with Shirley anymore."

Carrie stopped and looked at me, a little wisp of heat rising up from her collar.

"Or whatever," I said, slowing as we hit an icy patch, hoping I didn't fall on my ass. "Did you guys fight?"

"No." Carrie shrugged. "We're just . . . different people."

It's weird when you ask someone something and their answer gives you, like, no sense you've gotten an answer. Like a step sideways.

You were friends with this person for years, I wanted to say. How does that just end?

Instead, I asked, "What do you think she's freaking out about now?"

Carrie raised an eyebrow. "That's two questions."

"FYI, 'We don't get along anymore,' is kind of a half answer," I noted.

Carrie reached into her pockets. "It's probably something to do with Trevor. It's always Trevor. He loves her; then he doesn't. Most of the time, she's basically his doormat. He makes her half a person."

"Is *that* why you guys aren't friends anymore?"

"I don't know." Carrie stared at the sidewalk. "Maybe I was never her friend. Shirley is a super fucking selfish person, and maybe super fucking selfish people don't have real friends."

"But they have boyfriends?" I asked.

"Trevor is a *total asshole*," Carrie added. "He literally treats Shirley like garbage."

She shoved a second stick of gum in her mouth.

"He's so good looking," I said. "I don't trust boys that good looking."

Carrie punched me in the arm. Because I think she likes whacking my puffy coat. Admittedly, if someone else was wearing my coat, I would punch them, too.

"OW!"

It didn't actually hurt but still.

Carrie pulled out a packet of cherry from her left pocket and held it out. "I told you about Shirley. Now you tell me your thing."

I slipped a slice of surprisingly soft cherry gum out of the packet and unwrapped it with numb fingers. "I found a bag of money in my house."

Carrie popped a giant pink bubble. "Whose?"

I chewed to keep up. "My brother's, I think."

"How do you know it's his?"

"It was in his room."

Carrie popped another bubble. "Huh. Is that weird?"

"The bag or that I was in his room?" I ask.

"Both," Carrie said.

"Maybe?" I said.

Carrie shrugged. "Maybe he's thinking of making a run for it. Paying his way out of a sticky situation?"

"Maybe."

I thought of saying the thing about Todd and Mark lying about Todd, but then the bus showed up. Carrie shoved her hands in her pockets.

"Hey. Georgia. Just. You're not, you know," she added, as I stepped back so she could get past my big purple hemisphere.

"What?"

"You're not like Shirley," Carrie said, turning on her heel as she stepped up onto the bus and was whisked away. "You're like the opposite."

Now I'm home to an empty house. Which is pretty standard because my mom has yoga Wednesdays and my dad, as I think has been established, is never home. My house is a good house empty. It doesn't have any weird squeaks or banging noises, possibly because it's pretty new, paid for by either my dad's hard labor or my mom's creativity, depending on who you ask.

Home alone means I can eat my saltines on the couch and watch TV, so I'm huffing it up the stairs to get changed into my sweats when the house is suddenly full of the sound of my mom's voice getting shriller and shriller.

"You sit right there; you sit RIGHT THERE," my mom barks, stomping across the kitchen floor. "YES, HELLO? Yes. Yes, this is HIS WIFE. Tell him, no, I don't CARE; you TELL HIM to GET ON THE PHONE NOW. TELL him I just had to go to the SCHOOL and talk to the POLICE with his SON, and I need to talk to him NOW."

I peer through the hallway into the kitchen, where Mark is sitting at the kitchen table. His head down, his knee bobbing up and down in this way teenage boys do. I don't understand why.

My mom is pacing, the phone pressed to her ear.

I step softly into the kitchen. Mark looks up but only in this way that involves looking at me through the curtain of greasy hair. His eyes look tired. Like, really tired.

There's a puddle of snow water under the table, dribbling away from Mark's soaked sneakers.

"Hey," I whisper.

Mark shrugs and doesn't look up. "Hey."

Suddenly, my mom whips around and does that thing where she points UPSTAIRS with, like, a level of violence I don't think children's writers should ever exhibit.

I grab a sleeve of saltines and climb the stairs, listening. Mostly, all I can hear is my mom's tone. Which is at about a nine on the rage scale.

My dad gets home forty minutes later. Enough time for me to get to the bathroom and lie on the floor with my ear to the grate that connects to the kitchen.

"First of all, everyone just CALM DOWN."

"Do NOT speak to me that way, Will. I was the one who had to go to the school. YOU do not get to waltz in here and play some patriarchal role of—"

"I don't even know what's happening!"

"Tell him. MARK!"

Mumbling.

"MARK, speak UP."

"I . . . sort of cheated. On an exam."

"You SORT OF cheated? Explain to me how that is possible, Mark. To SORT OF cheat?"

"Sarah."

"WILL. Do not look at me like that. Our son CHEATED and I am ALLOWED TO BE ENRAGED."

Scooting on the floor. Chairs being moved.

I can see, without seeing, the big thick vein in my dad's neck, always covered with a thin layer of stubble, pulsing. It is the vein of frustration, the vein of disappointment.

More mumbling. Then my dad yells.

"GOD DAMMIT MARK, speak UP!"

"I said, I'm sorry."

My mom's voice cuts through my dad's hollering sharply. "The police were at the school. They think this has something to do with the boy who died. But no one is talking. Will, the POLICE are involved. They think this might have something to do with a MURDER."

My father's voice falls an octave. "What did you say, Mark?"

Silence.

"Nothing," Mark said.

"Is there SOMETHING you SHOULD say?" My mom's voice is so shrill it's vibrating the walls.

Mumbling again.

I can feel my heart thumping against the bathroom tiles.

"FINE. So we go to the police. You tell them everything you know. We go now."

"I can't."

My mom's voice is so high it's making the pipes shake. "OH YES YOU FUCKING CAN. OH YES YOU FUCKING CAN."

"It wasn't really cheating."

"OH, MARK!" my mom wails. "How stupid do you think we are? Principal Spot showed me your papers! You and your FRIENDS all answered the same question the same fucking way for FUCK SAKES."

"Okay fine! Okay. What do you want from me?"

The buzz of the fridge. A squeak of shoes.

"Tell me you had nothing to do with what happened to this boy."

"MOM!"

"TELL ME you had nothing to do with what happened to that boy, Mayer."

"Jesus, Sarah."

"Shut up, Will. MARK."

"I was HOME all night!"

"Mark—"

"I had NOTHING to do with it, okay? He was just. He was selling the answers, and I took them. That's it!"

My father's voice. Calm. "He sold them to you."

Thump.

The sound of what I could only imagine was my father's signature, if rare, palm slam on the table. Which I had only seen once before when Mark accidentally drove the car in the garage door.

"He was just some kid I got some answers from; it wasn't a big fucking deal. It was a mistake!"

"Let's go. Get in the car. Get in the car right now," my father's voice rumbles.

Steps echoing to the front door, which slams before I get downstairs.

I grab a jar of honey and sit at the table, dipping saltines and thinking.

Suddenly, I have this really clear memory. Of when Mark and I were kids. This one year, we stayed at my grandparents' place in Florida for a week during the holidays while my mom was on tour. It was this super retirement complex, and the pool had all these fancy rocks stacked on an island in the middle of the deep end. Because there was no one else under eighty to play with, Mark and I spent the whole week gathering "treasure" from the island. We'd swim to the platform in the deep end, reach up, and knock the rocks one by one into the pool, then we'd take turns diving down to "rescue" the rocks (my idea), put them in towels (Mark's idea), and carry them to my grandmother's backyard, tucked behind her gardening shed, where we were going to use a spoon to bury them once we had "enough." Possibly this meant all of them. After four days, we had pretty much cleaned the pool out, except for the giant pink stone I think was welded down.

Which is when this old man with like two hairs on his head and I'm going to say some sort of deadly facial rash, who was on the condo committee or something, freaked out and came knocking on our grandparents' door, because of course it was us. Old people don't steal rocks.

He had a baseball cap that said "BEST GRANDPA" on it, and he was, like, instantly yelling at us about the POOL GEMS. Even though we were just sitting all innocent-like in our grandparents' kitchen eating Cheerios. Like in his weird yellow grandpa flip-flops with his weird old-man toes waggling. He called us "degenerates."

My grandmother is not keen on confrontation. I thought she might melt into her sandals.

Meanwhile, I was terrified and started to cry. But Mark just stood up, and, still in his swim trunks, lead everyone to the back yard.

And pointed to the pile of white quartz glistening in the sun.

"There," he said. "We were going to bury them, but we'll put them back."

"Goodness," my grandmother said.

Later, my grandmother told my mother she blamed the whole thing on my mother's own "creative tendencies," which is a compliment hidden in a diss if you're coming at it from the right perspective.

And after that, we weren't allowed in the pool for the rest of the week. Which, by the way, a pool is the only reason you go to visit your grandparents in Florida. Not that I wanted to risk seeing the scary old man with the potato skin and weird sausage toes anyway.

I didn't ask Mark, who spent the rest of the week

looking for alligators on the side of the road, about why he fessed up until we were on the plane home, sitting in our vinyl seats with our bags of candy my grandmother got us from the airport.

"Why did you tell them?" I asked.

Mark put his headphones on and shrugged. "Because we did it," he said.

Because that's who he is, right? Like, no, Mark isn't some secret-agent, duplicitous asshole. He's someone who tells the truth when he's, like, directly asked about it maybe because it wouldn't occur to him to do any different.

And it hits me.

That's what the money is for! For answers. Like he said, he paid money to Todd to cheat on a midterm.

My mom sends me a text a few minutes later, tells me to heat up the meat loaf in the fridge.

And I do.

TODD
THE GAY APARTMENT

OF THE ROUGHLY SIX TIMES Todd visited Mr. McVeeter's apartment, he never saw it during the day. At least when he was alive.

In the light of day, the carpet of McVeeter's apartment was a glowing, vibrant red. The curtains were red, too, cherry red.

Blue was McVeeter's school color; red was his home color. Including the couch, the dishes, and the mug that was still out and half full of coffee on the gold coffee table. Red dishes McVeeter liked to serve brownies on with extra big mugs for hot cocoa he made from scratch.

"Guy is CLEAN," Greevy said, taking it all in. "Also this is a GAY apartment."

"And?" Daniels entered from the bedroom. "McVeeter is gay AND?"

"Well, we *knew* he was gay," Greevy scoffed, tipping over a frame on the bookshelf and looking at it. A picture of an old woman. "Makes sense his apartment is gay."

"Stereotypes," Daniels called back. "He's gay so he's clean?"

"Your house is spotless," Greevy countered.

Daniels stared at McVeeter's desk, at the collection of papers that were stacked up on either side of the ancient computer. McVeeter's desk was the only untidy part of his house, with various bits of paper left collaged without any rhyme or reason. He had his own personal filing system, notebook pages labeled with sticky notes with categories written in tall bright pink letters because he was getting nearsighted in his old age, he told Todd.

Every time Todd saw the desk, he had a strong urge to shove the papers back from the edge with his arm.

With a gloved hand, Daniels picked up a stray brochure for a gay cruise Todd was pretty sure McVeeter never went on. A karaoke cruise. Placed it back on the pile.

He pushed aside a few other bits before he came across something familiar to Todd, a notebook from McVeeter's desk. It was one of those cheap notebooks you get from CVS in packs of ten. A worn-out spiral ring notebook labeled MIDTERMS SS12 FALL.

"Midterm SS twelve." Daniels flipped open the notebook. "He handwrites them. There's a whole stack. Right on the desk."

"Which means if Todd were here, he could have gotten the answers," Greevy added.

"Or Todd could have gotten them from school," Daniels added. "McVeeter probably does some of this stuff at his desk at school."

"Hmm," Greevy said, disappearing into McVeeter's bathroom. "Maybe."

The search was Greevy's idea. She got the warrant. This was the lead, she'd said, she had a gut feeling now.

All the boys from Albright, all nineteen of the cheaters, eventually sang the same tune. Almost like they were just really good at following a lead or remembering lines to regurgitate on an exam.

After refusing to speak at school, Mark, with his parents on either side, his mother tapping her foot, sat in Greevy and Daniels' office later in the evening and told them that Todd had offered to sell them the answers to all the midterm exams for the year, for a thousand dollars.

Todd thought Mark looked tired. He kept his head down, his hands in his lap.

"A thousand?" Greevy looked at Daniels.

"That's a lot of cash." Daniels looked at Mark.

"He makes money shoveling driveways," Mark's father added, before pressing his lips back together in a grim fold.

"Where did he get the answers from?" Greevy asked each of the boys.

None of the boys knew, except Trevor. Perfect Trevor. Trevor with his blue eyes and his flawless neck. The morning after Mark fessed up, so early Greevy was still on her first coffee, Trevor arrived in Greevy's office with his back straight, like he was already sitting in the witness stand.

With his mother sitting next to him, in her white fur Todd thought made her look like a giant expensive bunny, Trevor spilled everything. The big confession.

"Todd told us," he said, "he could get the answers from McVeeter. He said he had some sort of connection to him. I can't remember what he said exactly.

And maybe I didn't believe him. But then he had the answers, and he told us all, he was, like, pay up."

"Pay up." It made Todd sound tough, which at one point he would have enjoyed.

Greevy wrote a tiny exclamation mark in her notebook.

Greevy got the search warrant an hour after Trevor left, and they were in McVeeter's apartment by early afternoon. Standing in McVeeter's living room, Daniels scratched his chin, as Greevy slid the notebook into a plastic bag. "The kids said they gave Todd money. A thousand bucks a pop, right? But we didn't find any in Todd's room. He's got a savings account balance of like eight hundred dollars and no deposits for the last month."

Birthday money Todd rarely spent.

"Maybe he had a deal with McVeeter," Greevy mused. "Maybe he gave the money to McVeeter."

"If he gave him cash, it's not here." Daniels paused. "Wait . . . you think they were working together? Because of what this Trevor kid said?"

"I don't know." Greevy looked around McVeeter's apartment. "Nineteen thousand dollars. Maybe. Teacher's salary—"

Daniels cut in. "But you also think Todd STOLE the answers from McVeeter."

"Look." Greevy touched the cigarette pack in her pocket with her free hand. "I fuckin' hate those snot-nosed kids at Albright, right? I thought they were little twerps and they were. They paid some nerdy kid they wouldn't talk to otherwise for answers to a midterm. They fessed up to being twerps and cheats. I got out of them what I expected. It fits."

"And?" Daniels folded his arms.

"And everyone's told us Todd had some sort of thing happening with McVeeter. McVeeter confirmed they had dinner together, which wasn't something he was doing with any other student. And they spent time together at school. McVeeter set up this tutoring thing and put Todd in charge of it."

"And?" Daniels didn't seem convinced.

Greevy clearly noticed.

"AND now we know Todd SOLD kids answers to a midterm he HAD TO have gotten from McVeeter. This Trevor kid says Todd got them from McVeeter. And, result, a bunch of kids have the answers to the exam. McVeeter must have SEEN that they were cheating when he marked the midterms BUT he said

NOTHING. So there's a piece there, right? There's something he's not saying. Right? Which is a pattern with this guy. Here we have something that could fuck with his job, and he says nothing? Kid dies. McVeeter says nothing. Why does someone clam up? When they know that telling the truth connects them to something bigger and more fucked up."

Watching the living was starting to feel like watching a TV show Todd couldn't turn off.

"Or he's a gay man, and he knows what you're thinking," Daniels said, looking at McVeeter's desk.

"What am I thinking?" Greevy's voice was suddenly steel.

Todd could picture what Greevy was thinking. What he assumed Mark was thinking when Mark told him about everyone knowing that he and McVeeter "had dinner," which made it sound like a date.

Todd and McVeeter.

Of course to even protest made the image all the more potent.

Todd and McVeeter, sitting in a tree.

Daniels frowned. "You're thinking he had some sort of inappropriate—"

"It's *already* inappropriate!" Greevy hollered. "What

was he doing hanging out with this kid outside of school?"

"Helping him? Because people at school were shit to this kid?" Daniels threw his hands in the air. "Look, he didn't tell us right away, but so far *he's told us* everything he did. ONE dinner. Working with him at school. None of that is—"

There was a knock at the door, and an officer stepped in. "'Scuse me," she said.

"What is it?" Greevy turned.

"There's a woman who says she saw the boy, here."

"She what . . . ?" Greevy's eyes went wide. "In *this* building? When?"

The woman lived on the second floor. The old lady with the silvery hair that McVeeter called a grand dame. She had three small dogs, all with what looked to Todd like bloody weeping tear ducts. She wore a brown fur coat that had little bits missing out the back, big black sunglasses, and big ancient-looking headphones, so Todd always assumed she was in her own world. A world that sounded like Sinatra and smelled like little white dog.

She walked her dogs, late at night. When Todd spotted her, it was on his second visit to McVeeter's apartment.

He'd stuck his foot in the elevator to hold the door open for the last little dog that was about to get splatted by the closing elevator doors. The doors slammed against the sides of his foot and sprung backward as the little dog yelped. The old lady turned and tipped the headphones off her ears and looked at him with what turned out to be an equally weepy looking eye.

And she said, "Thank you, young man."

Now the old woman was in the lobby, holding her crusty-eyed dog and talking to Greevy and Daniels.

"What a nice boy," she said to Greevy, ignoring the wimpering pooches at her feet. "A little thin. Needed a haircut."

"December," Daniels said, pulling out his notebook. "Do you remember what date?"

"Just that it was before the holidays," the woman smiled. "December something or other. Whatever night it was, it was cold as a witch's tit."

Daniels tapped his finger on his notepad. "Can I get your number, ma'am?"

The woman sniffed, took his pen, and wrote down her number in barely there strokes.

Greevy held the door open, letting the cold into the front hallway.

Daniels was already on the phone.

"He was a *nice* boy," the lady repeated, as she stepped out the door.

"He was HERE." Greevy slammed her fist into her open palm. "I'm calling forensics. We need to expand the warrant."

The day after Greevy and Daniels searched his apartment, another resident of McVeeter's building, who apparently spotted the officers by the elevators, remembered seeing Todd in the elevator the night he died.

This woman was in her twenties and lived on the floor below McVeeter. Todd didn't remember this woman. As she talked to Greevy and Daniels, Todd studied her features. She was tall and had lots of red curly hair she wore squished into a giant knitted hat. She said she passed Todd entering the building. She said Todd seemed preoccupied.

"Maybe not preoccupied." The woman chewed on her cheek. "Upset."

"Crying?" Daniels asked.

"Nah. Nervous," the woman said. "Like he was headed into an exam or something? I'm sorry, I figured someone else had already said something so I didn't call in. Also, I hate cops."

The woman scowled at Greevy, who smiled.

Maybe Greevy was smiling because this woman was sure the night she saw Todd was January 20. She was sure because it was the day before her birthday.

It took a few days to get prints back from the lab, but it was a jackpot for Greevy. They found a few partials in the living room and a thumbprint right on the doorjamb.

A big fat print, the tech said, delivering the news to the office in person. The skinny kid with the big fat print.

Looking at the report, Greevy beamed. The biggest smile Todd had ever seen her make. It was the first time he noticed how blinding white her teeth were, which was strange given how much she smoked.

Some things, Todd's ghost noted, just don't add up.

That night, after work, Greevy dragged Daniels to a bar called The Fox and The Badger to have a drink. It was a sticky-looking bar full of police detectives drinking beers in thick chairs with red vinyl seats. Greevy had a beer; Daniels had a whiskey. At first they drank in silence. Greevy spun a pack of cigarettes on the table.

"It's enough, right?" She spun the pack again before reaching for her beer.

"Maybe," Daniels muttered into his glass.

Greevy threw her arm out, nearly clocking a guy who was walking past her. "Daniels! Todd's fingerprints are all over the place. In the bathroom!" Greevy slammed her palm on the table. "He was there the night he died. You said McVeeter was on the up and up, and he wasn't! McVeeter LIED!"

"Yeah, I got it." Daniels checked his phone. His boyfriend. Texting with a grocery list.

Todd noted it was mostly wine.

After the bar, Daniels took a cab home to HIS gay apartment, which unlike McVeeter's gay apartment, was all gray curtains and carpet. His boyfriend was making pie in his underwear and a pink T-shirt with a panda on it.

"All pie, no pants!" his boyfriend cheered when Daniels walked in, doing a little dance.

Daniels's boyfriend was silly, Todd thought. Tacky, more like the kind of person who has brightly colored curtains and carpet. He made Daniels smile.

Daniels walked into the kitchen. He wrapped

his arms around his boyfriend and hugged him for a long time. His boyfriend was shorter so his head hit Daniels's chest, and Daniels's arms were long so they circled his boyfriend completely.

"What's wrong," the boyfriend murmured into Daniels's shirt. "Horrible day? Horrible world?"

"Something like that," Daniels said.

And Daniels kissed his boyfriend in the kitchen with weird dance music playing in the background.

Watching that kiss, Todd's ghost felt like something falling apart along very fine fissure lines, which is impossible for a ghost, which are matterless and, most of the time, without feeling.

Maybe if a ghost gets one regret, other than the overall regret of being dead, Todd's was that he died without ever kissing anyone he loved.

Of course, this didn't mean Todd hadn't ever kissed anyone (two boys, one with tongue and one without, and a girl named Marigold who sort of really just kissed HIM one summer at camp). It also didn't mean Todd had never LOVED anyone.

He died loving his mother and his father (in a weird, complicated way a person loves a person they don't really know). He loved his aunts. He loved his grandmother on his mother's side but not his father's.

And, as maybe only one other person in the whole world knew, he died *in* love.

That was the real secret, kept so close to the chest it pinched his ribs, a secret he kept on ice until he was ice.

Maybe there was a certain kind of ghost that dies that way. With love a whirr—fluttering like a trapped monarch in your chest as your heart beats its last accompanying beats.

GEORGIA
TWO PEOPLE EATING PANCAKES

IT'S SNOWING.

It started this morning, little pebbly flecks like grains of sugar that brushed against the window.

By French in third period, it was really snowing, collecting against the window while we wrote down what we ate for breakfast, in French.

"*Je mange rien*," Carrie said. "*Le breakfast c'est le big scam.*"

"I don't think 'scam' is French," I said.

Carrie drew a giant face on her paper with a giant open mouth with a coffee cup hovering over it. "What did you eat?"

"*Crêpes*," I said.

"You had *crêpes*?" Carrie looks impressed.

"*Crêpes* is French for pancakes," I said. "I had pancakes."

My dad made pancakes, because my dad and my mom are taking turns being home all day to watch Mark, who is the most grounded a person can be. They took away his television and his phone. So he spends most of his time reading. I think. Who knows what he's really doing in his room.

The pancakes were to try and make things feel less weird possibly, but like every gesture created to make things less weird, they really just make things more weird. Like when was the last time my dad made everyone pancakes, and we all sat at the table watching him read the paper like it was Sunday? When I was six? Never?

"I'll just write *crêpes*, too," Carrie said, shaking her pen back to life. "We both ate *crêpes*."

She draws another mouth dropping in from the top of the page, my giant mouth, biting into a giant pancake that takes up the whole middle of the page.

Carrie et Georgia mangez les crêpes.

After school, Carrie is at my locker. I spot the bag of money still in there but leave it behind, putting on my coat.

"Where are we going?" Carrie asks.

"I wanted to go to the park," I say.

Carrie frowns. "The park? What park?"

"Where they found Todd Mayer."

Carrie steps back. "Why?"

I don't have a good reason. "I can go by myself," I say.

"No, it's fine." Carrie turns, heading toward the door. "Let's do it."

Now it's snowing hard. Wet flakes that stick and stack so the street is a river of slush that sucks you in with every step. As soon as we get away from the main road and turn down the little residential streets that wind their way toward the park, the snow turns into a buffer, coating everything in quiet that makes every breath a sound as big as a word.

The park is empty. Just a single line of dog prints that cut through like a zipper. Even the trees are full of snow thick like white paint.

I can't remember where the police tape was, where they found Todd. If I did, it would probably be impossible to see anyway.

It's like everything is being erased.

"Okay," Carrie says quietly. "We're here."

Yesterday, they arrested a teacher at Albright for Todd Mayer's murder. It was on the local news. Reporters mobbing this guy with a sweater over his face as two officers lead him to a cop car. He was wearing a Bette Midler concert T-shirt, which to me was mostly weird because it must have been freezing outside.

My mom, sitting next to me, said, "Horrible."

"Let's go sit on the swings," Carrie says, pointing to the play area.

We slip-slide down into the basin of the park. Little-kid playthings all covered in ice and a few layers of snow—enough to make them mostly unplayable. The swings are stiff, and it's a struggle to get my big, puffy coat between the two chains, but I manage.

Carrie leans back in the swing, like she's waiting for a push or some sort of movement. "So," she says, "did you figure out the thing about the money?"

"I'm pretty sure it was Mark's money for paying Todd Mayer for answers to a midterm," I say. "He told my parents he cheated, and I guess they all had to pay like hundreds of dollars. So."

"Huh." Carrie steps back, still in the swing, as far as the chains will let her. "Fuck."

"Trevor Bathurst cheated, too," I say, which I know from eavesdropping on my parents. "The whole class cheated."

"Bet you a thousand dollars it was Trevor Bathurst's genius idea," Carrie says, lifting her legs so she's airborne.

"Yeah, I don't think it was Mark's idea," I say. "It's all so fucking pathetic. It's like actually the most pathetic thing ever."

Carrie's shoes skim through the snow under the swing. "What would you have done . . . if he was like actually involved? Like if he had something to do with what happened to Todd?"

"Is this a riddle?" I ask, twisting in my swing.

"No, it's a moral question." Carrie swings.

"I don't know," I say, honestly.

"Would you have gone to the police?"

I put my hands on my stomach. "No. But . . ."

I stand.

"I don't think I could ever look at him."

"Even though you didn't even know Todd?" Carrie asks as her swing slows to a halt. "You would, like, disown your brother over someone you don't even know?"

"I mean, I love my brother," I say, stamping in the

snow. "I don't *know* Todd. I wouldn't stop loving my brother. Obviously. But if he killed someone and then lied about it. Like even just lying about knowing Todd. It's just gross."

"I think it's the sort of thing people lie about," Carrie says. "That's why police are all, like, 'Where were you?' because they need facts to cut through all the lies people tell."

"Sure."

There is a moment of silence. Carrie leans back in her swing. "Do you remember in grade six? The cards Shirley and I handed out?"

"Yeah."

Of course I do. They were little cards with all our faults written on them. Shirley Mason's neat hand-writing, little white cards. We all had to line up at the swing set to get them. So we could improve ourselves, Shirley said.

Mine read: *Everyone hates it when you talk about yourself all the time.*

"It was Shirley's idea," Carrie says, still swinging. "I can't remember why. I think her mother is kind of fucked up and critical, which is why she's like that. Like she hates herself so she has to be mean to everyone else.

And she was like, 'Oh, okay, we can tell other people what's wrong with them.'"

"Okay." I don't know what else to say.

Carrie abruptly stops swinging. "It was her idea but I helped her and that's fucked up. But like, at the time I just thought, like, I was supporting my friend. Like there's so much of my life I fucking regret, and it's all stuff I did for someone else."

I still don't know what to say. "Okay."

"So, I'm sorry," she says. "For one. That I was, like, a part of that."

"Thanks. But." I'm confused. "My brother didn't do this, Carrie. I mean. He cheated. So I guess—"

Carrie stands. "I'm just saying. I know he didn't do it, and that fucked-up teacher killed Todd Mayer. Just. Like, maybe with this cheating thing, give your brother a break for doing something stupid for Trevor Bathurst. Like. Shirley Mason is the strongest person I know, and she would basically walk on glass for him. I'm just saying we're all . . . pathetic."

It's still snowing. Flakes are collecting in Carrie's hair.

I lean on the cold pole of the swing set. "You're not

pathetic. You're just a toothless school girl who refuses to wear proper winter boots."

Carrie smiles, then looks at her phone. "I gotta go; it's, like, almost six."

By the time we leave the park, ours are the only two sets of footprints leaving the scene of the crime.

At dinner, we're all sitting together eating Chinese takeout when my dad's phone rings and it's the guy who runs the driveway-clearing business who can't get ahold of Mark because Mark's phone is in a drawer somewhere.

"Mark!" My dad comes back in the dining room and slaps his phone down on the table. "Get your gear on."

Mark, who's been totally quiet the whole dinner, looks up. "What?"

"Get your coat. That was Mr. McNally. They need you to help clear a couple of driveways."

Mark puts his chopstick on the table, quiet. "I can't."

My mom, who's been on her phone for most of dinner, partly because she's rescheduling the release of her next book, sits up. "Why not?"

"I'm grounded," Mark says.

"You can still shovel a driveway," my dad says.

I slide a greasy spring roll off the plate and dip it in orange goo. Which seems like a very weird thing to be doing given the metric tonnage of eye-staring weight that's happening over the table.

Mark shoves his chair back from the table. "Fine, I don't *want* to shovel driveways."

"Then go to your room," my dad says.

What's more awkward than watching someone who isn't a little kid go to their room? It's like watching Mark fold in on himself. Which is pretty much how he's been all week. Like a big shadow of a person who both takes up the amount of space he takes up but somehow that space weighs nothing.

After dinner, I walk up to his door with a spring roll in a bag as a peace offering, and knock.

"Can I come in?"

"Yeah."

Mark sits up in his bed, which is a sea of books he's supposed to be studying from. "Thanks, but yeah, I can't eat that."

"Right," I say, putting the bag behind my back. "Uh, Mark?"

I lower my voice. "I have the money. For the exams? I found it. In the . . . house? I can bring it back."

I don't know what I'm expecting him to say. I don't know if I'm expecting him to be mad. I think about the kid who showed that angry man in Florida our pile of quartz. It's like I'm that kid now, but I'm not that kid?

"Yeah," he says, with equal quiet.

"It's your money," I say. "I don't know why I took it. I'm sorry."

"It's okay," Mark says. "It's not my money."

"Okay, well, I'll bring it back."

"Okay."

I walk away with my cold spring roll in its greasy bag.

I take out the trash to be helpful and to stand in the snow for a second under the light of the moon eating the cold spring roll that isn't against my training dietary restrictions. I can hear my parents in my mom's study arguing, which they generally don't do in front of us.

I am that super dense Molly kid in the book. All I have are questions that maybe aren't even the right questions.

Like who cares if Mark lied about Todd? Kids are shitty and mean. People are friends and then they stop being friends with the shitty people that made them do shitty things, and that's just how it is, right?

But then . . .

Why did Todd die? Like, really just because of some teacher? Why would his teacher kill him? It's like there's always some whole other layer of fucked up you don't even know to ask questions about because you don't even know it's there.

I stomp back inside. The house is almost as quiet as the park now as I kick off my boots and line them up with the rest of the boot family in the hallway.

TODD
PINK

TODD'S FUNERAL WAS ON THE coldest winter day anyone in attendance could remember. It was so cold no one could stop talking about how cold it was. Like the cold took over everything, and it was all everyone could think about.

Almost everyone.

It was so cold the dogs that had shit all over the park where Todd died refused to leave their houses, that morning. They whined at the door but wouldn't put their tender paws on the cold stone on the other side of the threshold.

The sky was blue, and the trees chattered with icicles. The roads were turned ink, as black ice made them slick as oil and the cars driving into the church parking lot wibbled and wobbled like drunks making a graceful exit at the end of a long night. All Todd's aunts arrived in their mother's furs, rolling out of their huge cars like big burly bears with brightly colored hats. Todd's mother wore her mother's gray fox, a relic that Todd used to sneak into the closet and push his face against when he was little, like it was a very old, very still family pet.

That week, Todd's mother had packed up his things with his aunts. They put some of his things in boxes, carefully packed, things that Todd didn't care about, books he didn't even really like they treated like china. Labeled TODD. They put his clothes in a bag his Aunt Lucy drove to the charity box. His Aunt Laura took his knitting needles home. His mother stacked the boxes in the living room, where they were sitting when Greevy and Daniels arrived.

"Can't do the basement yet," his mother said, touching the side of the cardboard, tracing his name.

"It takes time," Daniels said.

Todd's ghost was fading. It started when his mother started taping up the boxes. It felt like the world was getting smaller or harder to see.

Greevy and Daniels had stopped talking about

him. They'd wiped his name off the whiteboard and replaced it with Jed Hollings, the name of a forty-two-year-old man who was found floating in a frozen pool in the suburbs by the babysitter.

Maybe Todd wasn't fading, maybe he was shrinking to a particle size of consciousness. Or maybe he was expanding, blending into the horizon, looking down on the last moments he would ever know. The end of his afterlife.

At the front of the church, Todd's mother had a giant photo of Todd from a trip to his grandmother's house in Newark. It was a cropped photo, the edge of his Aunt Lucy's hand in the bottom left corner. Todd's mother thought it was his favorite picture. Actually, in Todd's favorite photo of himself, he is six, at some theme park, wearing a purple knitted vest and a pair of orange pants. In that picture, little Todd is smiling and holding his arms out to display the glory of his outfit for the person taking the photo. The smile in this picture is not the fake smile of the photo Greevy and Daniels had. It is a real smile.

That purple vest was the best. It had pockets on the outside and on the inside. Todd used to think of it as his magic vest.

Still, the picture of him at his grandmother's house (the grandmother he liked) was nice. It was a house that always smelled like baked cheese, which isn't a terrible thing. It was a house with an attic where he could go to read. A house where he felt safe.

People filled the first pews, shuffling in with the film of cold still stuck to their coats. Talking about how cold it was. Most of them were Todd's mother's friends from church and the dental office where she worked. People who had already sent the cards that lined her fireplace, all the same pastel washes and warm sympathies.

Principal Spot and his wife came. His wife was covered in dog hair, and Spot was sweaty as soon as he stepped out of the cold and into the church. After the service, they both shook his mother's hand.

"Todd will always be a cherished memory at Albright," he said.

"I hope so," his mother said.

Despite the fact that the service was on a Saturday, no other Albright boys or teachers attended the funeral, which was not surprising to Todd, but his aunts were furious.

"It was on the *news*," his Aunt Lucy hissed.

"Hush," his Aunt Laura chided, pulling her fur closer.

Todd knew, because Greevy and Daniels had discussed it, that McVeeter was out on bail. He also knew that, on day of the funeral, McVeeter issued a statement in conjunction with an LGBTQ legal-rights group that had taken his case.

"My relationship with Todd Mayer was only ever professional. Todd was a brilliant student and also subject to bullying in school. While this has been swept under the rug, my identity as a homosexual man has clearly colored investigators' view of my connection with Todd. This is prejudice, and myself and my legal team will fight this in a court of law. I did not kill Todd Mayer. His killer is still at large. I hope Todd's killer is brought to justice, and I wish peace for his family. More than that, I hope Todd will be remembered for more than his death. He was bright and funny. He had a world ahead of him before it was taken away."

McVeeter did not attend the funeral. But he sent a wreath of pink roses, delicate and sweet, to the funeral home. His mother chose it, and a wreath of holly and ivy from his aunts, to place front and center along with Todd's picture. Not knowing who sent it, of course. She just liked the roses.

Todd knew the roses were from McVeeter because McVeeter was the only person he'd ever told about pink. About how he secretly liked pink.

It was on the night he took McVeeter's notebook from the apartment. And for most of the hour he was there, he was nervously searching the room with his eyes. But eventually, sitting on the couch, drinking cocoa, he just got to talking. The liking pink thing just slipped out, like his goofy school photo smile, and he instantly regretted saying it.

"Or whatever," he said. "I'm just saying. Like some pinks . . . aesthetically are fine."

"Fine?" McVeeter had raised an eyebrow. "What's wrong with pink?"

"Obviously, there are certain associations," Todd said. "It's a stereotype."

McVeeter gave out a belly laugh. "Listen to you, 'certain associations' and 'stereotypes.' Just because it's a stereotype doesn't mean you can't like it."

"It's just not exactly what I need right now," Todd clarified.

"I think someday you're going to wear lots and lots of pink," McVeeter said, putting on his apron, which was lime green. "Someday you're going to be in a place where you can wear pink all you want. And you won't give a fuck. And no one else will either."

"I'll live with all the pink people," Todd snarked, spotting McVeeter's desk and the piles of papers. "The happy pink people."

"You will," McVeeter said, taking a note from Todd's tone and turning suddenly serious. "You will, Todd. Life is not high school. You'll see."

Todd wondered, the way ghosts can wonder, if McVeeter thought he was going to jail.

The last thing Todd said to McVeeter was that he was sorry. Possibly this was the moment he left his big fat thumbprint, as he leaned in the doorway.

"I *am* sorry," he said.

It was late. The latest he'd ever been to McVeeter's. He was so cold that night, because he'd been walking around the block. McVeeter sat on his couch, looking tired.

McVeeter dropped his head. Todd wanted him to be mad. Maybe Todd wanted McVeeter to be mad at him. To yell at him. But he didn't. He just looked resigned.

Now his little roses leaned up against the white marble shelf where they put his ashes. It looked a lot like a school locker. Except everyone walked by and touched it with their fingers. Did the sign of the cross. Including the girl who stayed behind when everyone else was gone.

GEORGIA
LOSING IT

I'M DRUNK.

Apparently, I'm an easy drunk, too, because I've had, like, two glasses of wine. It was expensive wine, from a cellar in Carrie's basement that looks like a haunted house in the suburbs. It was expensive and red and old, but it's only two glasses so I am easy.

Which is good because life is hard, you know what I mean? Life is fucking hard. And complicated. And MESSY.

Drinking is easy.

Carrie's house is a rich person house. It has pillars and a giant front door. A front hallway with a marble floor. It feels cold and like someone just sold it or wants to sell it. There are fresh cut flowers on every surface, and all the paintings on the wall are oil, including a giant painting in Carrie's living room of her and her father and her mother and a Saint Bernard named Lucy who died when she was seven.

I'm never sure what to do at a person's house. Carrie turned on the TV, and we watched *The Omen* and ate chips for the first little bit.

"Do you have"—I looked around at all the fancy furnishes, the expensive places I could easily stain—"like, a napkin?"

"My mom has someone clean the house like every day." Carrie shrugged. "Don't worry about it."

She jumped onto the couch, and I curled up on the other side, picking up a bowl of Cheetos.

"Do you want to watch something else?" Carrie asked, when *The Omen* was over. We were sitting on the couch, a big puffy couch with a brocade finish that felt like braille. A flowery braille on an otherwise slippery fabric. Carrie tucked her toes in under the cushion.

So close I could feel how close to me her toes were. Like inches. Maybe an inch. Close.

I had never sat so close to anyone I liked as much as I like Carrie. It's like actual heat.

When I was fourteen, my mom realized I was gay.

Because I kind of told her. Maybe she always knew by the fact that I was always falling in love with my gym teachers and camp counselors. So one day I came home, and she had *The Incredibly True Adventure of Two Girls in Love* rented, like on a DVD. And she took me by the hand and brought me to the couch and she was so fucking happy she was like, "We can watch it together."

On that couch, on that night, I died.

My first death.

I had no idea what to say. I just hugged a pillow to my chest and tried not to breathe while I could feel my mom looking over at me. Clearly already penning an illustrated book about my sexuality.

And, like, just before the scene where they kiss, because yes, OBVIOUSLY, I had already seen the movie, Mark came downstairs.

Just. Hello. I've been GAY since I could click a mouse. There are lots of things I've seen. I've seen *Claire of the Moon* (which you don't need to see because it's terrible).

Anyway, Mark was just back from practice, and he sat down on the couch and saw what we were watching, and he said, "What is this?"

"This is a movie about two queer women," my mom

said, gesturing at me. "And we're watching it . . . for your sister."

Second death.

The screen, at that point, was just flickering blobs of light to me.

And Mark stood up and stepped in front of the TV so we couldn't see the screen anymore, and he looked at my mom and said, "Does Georgia *want* to watch it?"

"NO!" I screamed, and I jumped off the couch and I ran upstairs.

And my mom never asked me to watch a lesbian movie with her again. Although she did make a point of telling me later that it was a good movie. Like the whole thing was just something she wanted to watch the whole time.

Is that pulling someone up off the cliff? Maybe not.

After *Omen*, Carrie wanted to watch *Bound*. Which is a much better lesbian movie. Then she offered to get the wine out from her parents' cellar.

Now I'm drunk.

Twenty minutes into *Bound*, which I have also seen, I feel Carrie's foot touch mine. Then she sits up and shifts over. Grabs the blanket on the back of the couch and puts it over our laps. Because we're sitting right next to each other. And my heart is beating so hard I can feel it in my eyeballs.

And just when Violet and Corky start kissing on the screen, Violet with her breathy gasps and Corky with her fake butch lesbian swagger, Carrie turns and looks at me. She's not chewing gum. Her eyes are huge, and I realize that the room is dark except for the light on the screen. But I can see her face so clearly. And I can smell her shampoo, which smells like oranges.

"I'm not doing this because they're kissing," she says softly. Her lips are stained red. That's the last thing I notice before she leans forward, and I feel her lips touch mine.

Her kisses are slow. She opens her mouth and slips her tongue against mine. Which is maybe the most amazing feeling in the world.

And I die again.

She takes off my shirt and my tights, fingers that can unwrap a piece of gum in less than a second working fast. My bra. Like so so fast, I don't even notice the bra go before I feel her flesh on mine, which is so hot, it's like a hot-water bottle.

I'm losing it.

I'm having sex on Carrie's couch. The first time I've

ever had sex. This is what it's like. All I can feel is the surface of my body and the surface of hers. I can hear her gasping when I touch her, like whatever I'm doing is strange good but like it's not enough. I don't know what to do and I'm afraid to ask.

"Put your fingers," Carrie whispers. "Your fingers."

I've never felt anything like this. I don't even need her to touch me before my whole body explodes and then we're twisted on the couch, and *Bound* isn't even over yet.

Carrie curls up against me, her head a few inches from mine, the blanket twisted around us.

It takes me a second to realize her face is wet.

"Georgia."

"Are you okay?"

"Georgia."

She sniffs. I can feel the wet of her tears on the arm of the couch.

"Can you look at me?" she whispers.

"What?" I pull her close. Because I'm suddenly terrified this is all going to go.

"Can you look at me? Please?"

TODD
THE LAST DAY

IT WAS ALMOST TODD'S LAST day as a ghost. Which ghosts know.

Released from Greevy and Daniels, for whom he imagined he was now a piece of history, he spent most of his time in his mother's home. Where his mother slept on the couch next to his pile of boxes, the TV on all night, on the shopping channel because his mother was always afraid of waking up to silence.

After his funeral, Todd floated into his room for one last time, hovered over his bed, and wished things were very different for the millionth time.

You don't think about a lasting legacy when you're alive. When you're alive, you just think about what's happening in that moment. Because it's not your last thing. When you're alive, everything feels important. Every little thing. When you're alive, you don't realize what's actually big is the everything you leave behind. The whole story. A thing so big most people will never know it. Just pieces.

On the last day he was alive, before he "went to the movies," Todd had a frantic feeling the whole day. Like his stomach was a kettle boiling. Like his limbs were turning to jelly.

It started when Mark and Trevor cornered him during gym class and told him what they'd done with the answers. It had never occurred to Todd, when he first thought of it, that giving Mark the answers would result in anything more than Mark getting a better mark on his midterm. Of course, he'd realized that it was possible that Mark would share the answers with Trevor, because they were friends.

But he didn't know until that morning, standing in his too big gym shorts to a chorus of bouncing balls, that Trevor had sold the answers, answers Todd had copied from the notebook he stole from McVeeter's apartment and then stealthily returned while McVeeter made hot cocoa, to fucking EVERYONE.

The day of the midterm Todd HAD seen Chris

Mattieu before class reciting something that sounded like the answer to the essay question in the hallway, but he'd figured he was just being paranoid.

"You ALL"—Todd's knees were suddenly jelly—"MEMORIZED the answers? ALL of you?"

"Well, what did you think we would do?" Mark asked, seemingly genuinely.

"McVeeter will know." Todd gulped, rubbing his arms, his back pressed up against the white painted wall of the gym, overwhelmed by the sounds of basketballs slamming against the floor in the background.

"NAH," Trevor cooed. "McVeeter doesn't know shit. He thinks it was *me*, not that I was ever at that perv's house. He fucking lost his shit at me in the hallway."

Trevor looked at Todd when he said perv, a little bit of spittle bouncing off his lip.

"So he DOES know?" Todd tried to keep calm, keep cool. He was clearly failing.

"Don't worry about it," Trevor scoffed. "McVeeter can't PROVE shit."

"We have your cut of the money," Mark offered, upbeat. "I can meet you tonight and give it to you."

"I don't want any money." Todd tried to stand straighter.

"Aw." Trevor put his arm over Todd's shoulder and jostled him in an aggressive bro half hug, his funk enveloping Todd. "That's so sweet, Todd. Helping us out of the good of your heart."

"It's only fair," Mark pressed. "I can meet you tonight. With the money. Okay?"

Mark pushed his hair off his face, revealing the deepest, darkest brown eyes.

Todd loved Mark.

Ever since he walked into class in grade nine and sat down in front of him in bio with his giant body and his black mop of black hair. He had the nicest, deepest voice. A strong voice that went with his giant hands, in Todd's opinion. Todd used to think about what it would be like to hold Mark's hand. He'd imagine Mark squeezing his hand, like before they'd enter a room together. Like the squeeze you give someone to let them know everything is going to be okay.

Mark had shitty friends, but when he and Todd were together, alone, he was really nice. He was never funny, like in a telling jokes kind of way, but he always looked like he got Todd's jokes when they studied together, anyway. When Todd went to his house and Mark brought him up to his room that one time, they talked for, like, an hour not even about school. Just. They talked about everything, like, what it was like going to an all-boys school and this idea that kids who went to Albright were stuck-up assholes and what it meant that their parents were spending so much money to send them there. Mark wasn't even weird when Todd mentioned his mother's books, which Todd had always liked. Mark said he wasn't a big fan.

"It's just, like," Mark said, shrugging, "her version of things, you know? I, like, don't even read them anymore. My sister fucking HATES them."

Mark was the only person who made Todd smile, which was something he pretty much never did at school. You smile, and people know they have an in on you. They know they've got you.

And maybe Mark knew that he had Todd, because sitting in his room, he told Todd he was screwed.

"Just, like." Mark had sighed. "So fucking screwed."

He needed at least a high B grade in social studies for his college applications. His grades were bad. Todd offered to tutor him more, but Mark said he had practice and he was worried. He couldn't afford to screw up. He couldn't take the chance.

"I worked, like, four years to get on the team and

get better and now, like, if I don't get better grades it, like, doesn't even matter? It's, like, what the fuck am I going to do?"

No one had ever asked Todd for help before. And really before that moment, it wasn't like Todd was really in a place to help anyone. Todd was not a person people asked for anything other than a pencil. But he had been to McVeeter's house. Seen the desk with all its papers.

"I could get the midterm answers for you." The words just slipped out of his lips.

"OH DUDE! Really? Holy shit."

Todd thought maybe Mark would hug him but he just collapsed backward on his bed with a huge sigh of relief. "Holy shit. That would be really amazing."

Todd agreed to meet Mark that night because he wanted to see him. Without Trevor. Alone.

The night he died, Todd's plan was to tell Mark that he was going to turn himself in. Then, the next day he was going to tell McVeeter he stole the test questions and the whole thing was his idea.

He knew if he told McVeeter, McVeeter wouldn't tell Spot. But at least he wouldn't be lying. He would tell the truth, and McVeeter would protect him.

He wasn't actually planning on going to McVeeter's

house that night, but at the last minute Mark called and said he would be late meeting at the park. And McVeeter's apartment building was right there. And everything was closed. And it was cold. And Todd thought he would get it over with. So he walked over to McVeeter's building. And he knocked on McVeeter's door.

"It was *me* who stole the test," he said, not leaving the doorway, his neck getting warmer and warmer in his recently completed knitted scarf. "But I need you to keep it a secret."

"It was you," McVeeter repeated. He seemed surprised but not too surprised.

He walked back into his apartment and turned on the kettle. "Are you coming in?"

"No, I-I just," Todd stammered. Tried to quiet his voice. "I just need to know y-you're not going to tell on me."

"I'm not." McVeeter sighed, wiping crumbs off the counter. "I could be in as much shit as you about this, Todd."

Todd breathed a sigh of relief. "Okay so. Okay. Thanks."

"Todd." McVeeter looked over at him, heavy. "Friends don't ask friends to do this kind of thing for them. Trevor Bathurst . . . I know you didn't do this on your own."

Todd stiffened.

"I didn't say a friend—it wasn't for a *friend*," Todd said. "I'm sorry I did it. It was for me. Okay? I'm sorry."

McVeeter sunk into his couch. And said a bunch more things that blurred together. And then Todd stepped out, closed the door behind him.

And in that moment, Todd was happy. On the last night of his life. He felt suddenly light. Because they were off the hook. Mark and Trevor wouldn't get in trouble. Mark would get into college, because of Todd.

And he was going to see Mark.

He burst out the doors of McVeeter's building and into the frozen night, smiling as he practically skipped over the salt pebbly sidewalk to the park where a boy he liked was waiting for him.

In this park, Todd's ghost thought, settling over the white space where he died.

In this park.

Right.

Here.

GEORGIA
PIZZA

AS SOON AS CARRIE STOPS talking, I run and throw up in her parents' bathroom, which is completely mirrored. So when I look up, I get a full view of my vomiting from every angle.

After that, I throw up on Carrie's parents' walkway, next to a set of manicured tiny bushes capped with snow.

Next, a cab ride later, I throw up on my walkway, next to the glowing candy canes my mom still needs to take down. This is where I get to see that my barf is purple and orange. Wine and Cheetos.

The driveway is empty. My parents' car is gone. Saturday night date night.

Inside, the house feels empty. I trip over the bodies

of soggy shoes in the front hall and immediately my stomach flips and I run and throw up in the sink in the kitchen, which is mercifully dark. I hear a creak and spin around, and Mark appears in the doorway, snapping on the kitchen light, which burns my retinas.

"Are you drunk?"

I lean on the counter. "Where's mom and dad?"

"At dinner. Look, Trevor is getting pizza." Mark shrugs. "He's just here for dinner then he's going. Okay?"

"You're not allowed to have people over." I wipe the barf from my lips with the back of my hand. The thought of pepperoni makes my stomach flip, and a burp hops out of my mouth. A wet one.

"He won't be here for like . . . ," Mark grumbles, sitting down at the kitchen table. "It's just a visit. He's my friend, G, chill out."

"Oh, HE'S your friend."

I look down at my feet, which are pooling water, on the floor. Gray rivers. I'm wearing the boots Mark gave me because he got new ones. My feet are shoved into them because I ran out the door while Carrie was still yelling behind me. So the tongue of the left boot is squashed up against my big toe. They're too big. Really. I should get my own boots. But I think a part of me wanted these because they were Mark's. Maybe because of our ages and genders, there weren't a lot of Mark's things that I got as a kid. The odd winter coat. A set of mittens. All protective layers.

"Where are your winter boots?" I ask.

"What?" Mark coughs.

"Where are your WINTER BOOTS," I yell.

"I lost them." Mark takes a sip from a can of pop on the table.

"Hodo you lose your boots?" I slur.

"You just do." Mark frowns.

"When did you lose them?"

This is what I have been thinking about since Carrie started talking, spilling her guts to me, on the couch. This is what I have been thinking about since I started puking: Mark's boots.

Mark looks up through his bangs. "Why do you care about a fucking pair of boots?"

"Because I think . . ." I steady myself. "I think you didn't have your boots since after Todd died."

"I fucking lost my boots." Mark stands, suddenly obviously taller and stronger than me. "You're giving me shit for losing my shit when you went INTO MY ROOM and stole money from ME."

"I know," I say, stepping back. "I know what happened."

"G." Mark's voice gets low, subterranean. "Just. Don't—"

I want to puke again. "Don't what?"

"G. Please." Suddenly, he looks scared. I want him to look angry again.

There's the crackling of tires on the driveway, the pop of inflated rubber on snow on asphalt.

"Georgia." Mark's face is white.

"I FUCKING KNOW EVERYTHING," I scream so it makes me feel even more hollow than I probably am at this point.

Just as the door bursts open and Trevor yells in, "Hey what's—"

"FUCK YOU I FUCKING KNOW EVERYTHING!"

"Georgia!" Mark's voice sounds like I'm falling. Like I've tipped back and he's watching me fall.

I bolt up out of the kitchen, my feet slipping on the floor, making me fall into Mark's arms. Like hitting a brick wall. I shove him away as I feel his fingers trying to grab my sleeve.

"Georgia!"

"What the fuck?" Trevor's voice cuts through my blur.

I hear the pizza box clatter down on to the table, rattling the salt and pepper shakers shaped like a paintbrush and tube of paint.

"FUCK YOU YOU FUCKING MURDERERS!"

I run, through the hallway, to the stairs, suddenly lost in my own house because I meant to run outside. My head feels like it's going to pop. I can hear footsteps, huffing, behind me as I run up the stairs. I'm halfway when I hear a *whump whump* of feet, and I feel a hand wrap around my ankle, tight. The hand squeezes, yanks my foot back, and I fall forward, my other foot slipping off the stair so I'm briefly airborne, then, before I can blink, I feel my chin hit the stair with a CRACK. Something is broken. Sharp and warm fills my mouth in a wave.

The hand on my ankle pulls harder, yanking like I'm a fish on a line.

I hear Mark yell, "TREVOR!"

I can taste blood. It's pouring down my chin. I can feel Trevor's grip vibrating.

I'm going to die.

"STOP!"

Die for real.

"TREVOR!"

The hand lets go. I roll on my side, spit and blood comes out, soaking the already soaked carpet on the stairs beneath my chin. Somewhere outside my throbbing head I hear muffled voices yelling. I hold my hand up to my mouth and spit a piece of tooth onto my palm, a little white triangle like a piece of a tea cup. White on red.

I look up and see Mark holding Trevor in what must be some sort of wrestling choke thing, from behind. He's dragging Trevor backward as Trevor kicks out and tries to get free, his face a blur of red and blond.

"Fucking asshole." Spittle sprays out of Trevor's lips.

"FUCK YOU!" Mark's face is red.

As I try to get to my feet, I turn and see Trevor's eyes bulging, against the hold of Mark's arm. I fly up the rest of the stairs, my fingers grabbing for each stair, the smell of blood filling my nose as I scramble into my room and slam the door behind me.

I'm making noises I don't understand. It's like someone's choking an animal in my room, but it's me as I scramble to grab a chair and shove it against the door.

I'm up against the wall next to the door, breathing bubbles of yuck, when I realize I should call the police. When I hear footsteps on the other side of the door. Heavy breathing.

"Georgia? Are you okay? Georgia?"

"Go away," I cry. "I'm calling the police."

There's a scraping sound, sliding down the other side of the wall.

"Okay. Okay, G."

"DON'T COME IN HERE!" My hands are shaking and sticky. I can't unlock my phone.

"Georgia. It was an accident. I swear it was an accident."

"FUCK YOU! You fucking LIAR!"

"G. I promise. I didn't. It was an accident. He fell."

TODD
LAST STAND AT PEACOCK PARK

MARK WAS ALREADY THERE WHEN Todd got to Peacock. Other than Mark, the park was empty, not even the echo of a pug. Todd punched over the parts of the snow that were smooth and untouched on his way up to the swing set. Mark was on the swing. He stood up, his coat pressing up against the chains of the swing as he did.

"Too tiny." Mark pointed back, as he stepped forward toward Todd. "For me."

"Yeah," Todd said. "I mean swings always made me sick. So."

"Not a swing guy." Mark smiled. His cheeks were all rosy.

Todd imagined what it would be like if they were

just meeting in the park. Like if this was where they hung out. Like, what if that was what he and Mark did. Late-night walks under the stars.

"Yeah, not my scene," Todd said, trying to sound relaxed.

Mark's breath came out in soft little plumes. Like down feathers puffing out of his mouth.

"So." Mark stepped forward again. "Uh, sorry I'm late. I mean, that I had to change . . . the time. I needed to wait for my parents to crash."

"It's cool," Todd said. "I actually, I had some stuff to do. Late-night errands."

"Yeah?" Mark smiled again.

"Yeah," Todd scoffed, "just picking up some butter and some . . . paperclips."

Mark smiled again, but it looked nervous this time. "Right," he said.

He pulled his glove off with his teeth and reached into the pocket on the front of his coat, which Todd figured had the money in it. Todd held up a mittened hand.

"Uh hey. I'm not taking the money," Todd said. "I didn't know, okay? I didn't know you were selling them. I'm actually, sort of against that sort of thing?

Personally? But, it's fine and I'm not mad. But . . . I didn't get the answers to sell them."

Why did he say he was against it? Who's *for* selling answers? Is that a thing a person is for? Obviously, Mark and Trevor were for that sort of thing. But Todd thought, hoped, it was Trevor's idea. Not Mark's.

"I got them for *you*," Todd added. His voice sounded dangerously earnest.

A frozen wind whipped the little bits of loose snow up into the air, blowing right through Todd.

Mark paused, his hand still in his pocket. "Oh, uh."

Todd felt himself blush, which he knew would give him not rosy cheeks but a series of state-shaped red blotches on his face, over the bridge of his nose. "I mean, to help you out. Because you needed it."

Mark pulled his hand out of his pocket. "I think, *Trevor* and I would just feel better. If we all shared this. You know?"

That's when Todd realized that *Trevor* wanted to be able to say that *Todd* took the money. Because he was setting him up, Todd thought. Trevor. But not Mark. Maybe not Mark.

Suddenly, Todd was weak.

"Well," Todd pressed his lips together, spoke with

what he hoped wasn't a quivering voice, "I don't want it. And I'm not doing it again. I told McVeeter—"

Mark's eyes bugged out. "You told McVeeter! What did you tell him?"

Mark's voice cracked in the cold air.

"I didn't want him to keep looking for who did it. And I didn't want to lie!" Todd's voice squeaked in comparison, like a dog's yip. "I told him it was *me*. Just me. I—"

"Fuck, Todd," Mark shook his head. He pulled out his phone with his bare hand. "Fuck."

"What are you doing?" Todd stepped forward.

"I'm just . . . calling someone," Mark said, mumbling as he tried to dial with his glove. "Fuck."

Todd didn't know what to do next. He just didn't want Mark to call Trevor. He just wanted to talk to Mark. Alone. To explain that McVeeter wasn't going to do anything. And so he stepped up to Mark and put his hand on Mark's arm, not to take his phone or anything, just to stop him for a second. Mark was like a brick wall, like there was no bend to him as Todd tried to gently push his phone arm down. In a fuzz of action, Mark yanked his arm up to pull away.

"HEY!" Mark yelled.

Todd saw Mark's elbow swing toward him and whipped his head back. His feet hit a patch of ice and slipped out from underneath him.

And he saw the sky, black with Christmas light stars, and then his head slammed into what felt like a baseball bat, but was probably the post of the swing set. Whatever it was, it was like a rock.

And then nothing, except a weird soft tunneling backward. And then nothing. And nothing but a chill creeping in from the edges of Todd's increasingly shrinking reality.

And then, how much later Todd couldn't tell, a voice.

Two voices. Girl voices. One sharp and frantic.

"Holy fucking shit! Is he dead? Fuck! What the fuck!"

One calm and low. Close.

"Just relax, okay?"

Todd couldn't open his eyes all the way. But he could see a sliver of a face. Of the arm of a gray coat.

"Can you hear me?"

"FUCK, Carrie. Just. Fuck, let's GO! Please? Carrie! Please!"

"I'm going to get help. Okay? I promise."

"Let's GO!"

His head hurt. But by then it was just a little hurt. Like something several blocks away but important, a disappearing siren. He tried to open his mouth. But it felt like a steel trap. Like when his garage door used to stick and he and his mom would yank on it and it wouldn't budge. So Todd fell back into himself. Let the darkness take him.

And then he was a kite in a dark place, being pulled through a black bumpy storm that was all texture and no shape. Noises like thunder, low rumbling thunder.

Todd's ghost hovered over the spot where he took his last, soft shallow breath.

Compacted in the space of that breath was the cacophony of Todd's existence: all the things he was and wasn't. Bad things like the sound of his footsteps on the marble floor at Albright, good things like the sweet sound of knitting needles slipping and knotting wool into a line. Somewhere in that space, at its nucleus, was a pinprick of a memory that was better than it deserved to be, of the first time Todd made Mark laugh with a joke, about soup.

We don't pick the things that end up in our last breaths.

We just breathe them.

Out.

The moon climbed into its favorite spot in the sky, where it was a window in the night, and Todd was gone.

GEORGIA
TODD

HEY.

So.

This is your place now, huh? Who knew mausoleums were so chilly.

Cold but classy, by the way, in case you were worried.

I think you're the only kid in your block. Most of the ash pots have little black-and-white pictures next to them, grandmas and grandpas. An "Aunt Marcie" that looks pretty gay to me. There's at least two sets of plastic flowers in your row.

So maybe not so classy.

Your ashes are in a little white urn that looks like someone pulled the label off a can of soup and painted it white, which is cool. Definitely different. There are little shriveled rose petals on the ground in front of your locker thing that look like confetti. Also, someone's taped a pink ribbon to your little window.

I wonder if you hate the fact that you're basically in a locker. Which is maybe like being trapped in school for the rest of your life. Your afterlife.

Or you're dead, so maybe you don't care.

In case you're wondering what's going on with my face, I have six stitches below my bottom lip, which actually itch like fucking crazy. (It used to be seven stitches—but I pulled one out in my sleep.) When your fellow student Trevor Bathurst grabbed my foot and I hit the stairs with my face, my front teeth went right through the flesh right below my bottom lip. I cracked my bottom tooth and punched out my top front tooth. I look like one of those pictures from an ad where someone has blacked out one of the teeth with a ballpoint pen. I've spent two days at the dentist getting things pulled and filed, although I was completely high for the whole thing.

On the drive home, my dad said, "Wish I was getting knocked out."

Oh yeah and the thing that looks like a kid's pirate

beard under my chin, is the leftover bruise from where my chin hit the stair, and the splint is because I also broke my pinky finger somehow. I look like I've been in a fight.

I mean, I guess I have.

At least I managed to kick Trevor in the face, which I don't remember doing but when the police talked to him, apparently he had a broken nose and he told the cops I assaulted him. So. Good for me. Mark broke his arm wrestling Trevor to the ground.

Saving me. I guess.

So I suppose I'm here because I wanted to tell you in person how you died.

The whole thing.

After the fight and the barfing and the police coming to my house and everything, Carrie went to the station, and she told the detectives what she told me.

She said that on the night you died, Shirley was sleeping with Trevor, because they were on again and off again, which maybe you knew?

Anyway, they're mid bone, and he got a call and ran off. And Shirley was mad and she thought Trevor was cheating on her, right, again I guess, so she followed him in her fancy SUV. But then when she got to the park, she saw Trevor and Mark getting into Trevor's car. And they were arguing. And Shirley got scared. She said she thought it was drugs, and so she called Carrie, her best friend, her former best friend, and told her she was at the park and she needed help.

And so, at like midnight or something, Carrie takes her dad's car and sneaks out and goes to the park because Shirley was so freaked out. And they went up to the playground and that's when they found you. Lying in the snow next to the swing set. There was lots of blood and your eyes were closed. And Shirley thought you were dead. And Carrie thought you were alive.

And Carrie wanted to call the police, but Shirley was scared. And she was in love with Trevor. And she was all, like, what if something happened to Trevor? And Carrie realized Shirley is the least intelligent person ever and after that they stood in front of Shirley's car in the park parking lot and screamed at each other until Trevor and Mark came back and Trevor told them you were dead.

Trevor told them if they didn't leave, they would *all* get arrested for murder. And Shirley was, like, so happy to see Trevor not cheating on her. And she begged Carrie to just go home. Like it was no big deal, and Todd was dead so they should *all* just go home, like Trevor said.

And Carrie said she was, like, you asked me to come here. What the fuck?

And Shirley was, like, it was a mistake. He's dead. Just go home.

So Carrie left.

She left you there.

That's what she told me that night after, not that you care, but OKAY after the first time I ever had sex, the person I had sex with told me that she saw you in the snow, BLEEDING, and she left you there because Shirley and Mark and Trevor told her to.

Even though she thought you were alive.

Even though she said she told you she was coming back.

She didn't.

I just really, really hope you didn't hear her that night.

That's actually something I think about a lot, is you hearing Carrie say, like, everything's going to be okay.

And then her doing nothing.

She drove home and got into bed. And she told herself that you were dead. She said Mark said it was an accident. She thought they were just going to leave your body there. She didn't know that Mark and Trevor had gone to Trevor's house to grab garbage bags because they were going to take off all your clothes and drag you into the woods.

That's what Mark told the detectives and our parents (while I was in the other room, listening). Mark said they wanted to remove your clothes in case there was evidence because I guess Mark watches crime TV shows, too.

Although I guess they left your mittens behind, which someone's dog found the next day. So. My brother is a sloppy criminal is I guess what I'm saying.

Apparently, you had pink mittens on you that night.

I don't know why I like that idea so much. I picture you knitting them. Not that I really know anything about you.

I do know that when Carrie talked to the detectives, they said you were mostly likely alive when Carrie and Shirley saw you. That you hit your head, but you died from the cold.

I mean so really, they all killed you, is basically what I'm saying. They could have saved you, but they didn't. Not Shirley, not Trevor, not Carrie, not Mark. None of them.

And I know it's not really your problem anymore, but I don't really know what to do with that.

Maybe it's not about me.

Or maybe it's about everyone in this bigger way I'm sure my mom will never write about, because it would be a super dark children's book, about how people do shitty things for shitty people when they would be way better off hanging out with less cool but much nicer people like you and me. (I'm assuming you're nice if maybe you were a little geeky and annoying.)

A week after she confessed, Carrie sent me this super long email. She told me what she told the cops, most of which I already knew. She also told me how horrible Shirley was and how Shirley was, like, so wrapped around Trevor's finger it was disgusting and pathetic.

She also said that she and Shirley slept together when she was fifteen.

This was in an EMAIL, okay? Which is probably evidence.

It feels like maybe Carrie was my friend because

I was the opposite of Shirley. And she was sick of Shirley's bullshit.

But also pretty fucking ironic that all the things she hated Shirley for a) being a user while being b) wrapped around someone's little finger, apply to her just as much.

I haven't talked to her since we slept together. Although she texts me every once in a while.

So yeah, I don't know what happens now.

I'm pretty sure Trevor and my brother go to jail, although they're out on bail. And maybe Carrie and Shirley will have to do community service or something?

I guess none of that changes the fact that you're dead.

And I'm here.

Alive.

Todd.

I'm sorry my brother was a jerk to you. I'm sorry he wasn't your friend. He fucking should have been. He should have saved YOU. I don't hate him, but I don't forgive him. I don't forgive any of them.

McVeeter is out of jail, so you know. Which is good. Although it's still fucked up that you can go to jail for something you didn't do. I wonder if he went back to Albright or, like, moved to New York or something. Whatever you do after something like this happens.

Anyway, maybe you already know all this.

Maybe you're already haunting the spot where Trevor and Mark burned all their winter stuff with your clothes afterward. To destroy all the evidence. They burned it in Trevor's backyard barbeque pit, so actually this is further evidence that they are lazy terrible criminals because the police found the stuff later. Your clothes, half burnt. They also found a piece of Trevor's winter coat that had blood on it. And a bit of Mark's boots.

At home, my mom is crying all the time and my dad has started smoking outside and the house is sort of crap and there's blood on the stairs still and everything is shit but mostly I know it's REALLY shit for you, because you don't get a chance to have anything be better than dead now.

But I do.

So there, Todd. That's the end of the story of you. A story I weirdly get to tell after having so much anxiety about someone else telling my story all the time.

Anyway, I'm going to try and learn something from it.

I promise.

I'll say this. You don't know me, but I've felt lost for so long but I don't feel lost now. I know where I am.

The snow is melting and I can hear the water rushing beneath the cliffs of snow in the cemetery. I can smell the green things getting ready to come up from under the ice. The sky is blue and bright.

I'm walking home, away from you but not forgetting you. Never forgetting you.

The sun is warm on my face.

ACKNOWLEDGMENTS

THIS BOOK TOOK FOREVER TO write, and it was written with the support of many.

Thank you to my editor Connie Hsu and everyone at Macmillan and Roaring Brook for helping make this book a reality and for being patient when I disappeared into the dark hole of this mystery.

I am forever grateful to my agent, Charlotte Sheedy. There is none like her. I am very lucky to have her in my corner.

A giant, emphatic thank you to Kim Trusty for her insight and wise counsel. Thank you to Ally Sheedy for being a lifeline. So much love to the writers and artists whose advice I have come to rely on these last few years, including Cory Silverberg, Nidhi Chanani, Justin

Hall, Minnie Pham, Michael V. Smith, Abi Slone, and Rainbow Rowell. All these people have taken at least one phone call and talked me down off at least one cliff.

Thank you to my therapists.

Thank you to my mom and dad, who made it possible for me to be this person, and then made it possible for me to be a writer by paying my rent for many many years.

Thank you to Heather Gold, my heart and home, the most amazing, funny, talented, and inspired person, the person who makes me want to be better and better, who helps me face the hard things, a process that has undoubtedly affected these pages.

This is a book about the death of a gay teen, a subject I in no way take lightly. This is also a book about survival and fighting for truth. For the LGBTQIA+ teens out there who have fought for their truths and their lives, really, this book is for you. If you can, and I hope you can, take your pain, turn it into art, live to tell the tale.

The Trevor Project is the world's largest suicide prevention and crisis intervention organization for lesbian, gay, bisexual, transgender, queer, and questioning (LGBTQ) young people. For support text START to 678-678, phone 1-866-488-7386, or go to thetrevorproject.org.